Left of the Middle

By Gary Hope

All the facts and stories and names in this book are true and accurate . . . even Dink.

"Left of the Middle," by Gary Hope. ISBN 978-1-949756-02-9 (softcover).

Published 2018 by Virtualbookworm.com Publishing Inc., P.O. Box 9949, College Station, TX , 77842, US.

One day you'll just be a memory to a few people. Do your best to be a good one.

Cleveidadorismaryjoeandyearlannielouherberhazelgcdonal
dettabillsusanshelleykaliannecaseymarkjonpauldotsaralin
dagailjudyconradjerrydickielarryallenredspringswinstonsal
emclemmonsirelandkillarneygalwaypembrokeappalachian
goodwilllusklanceehfairviewmattoxcoperiklefscurtisbaseba
lltravelsportsjesusjohnabbeypaulgeorgeduaneringomoabeli
zabethdinkamandacarterjoelailenmaireadjuliettemikedesm
ondclaireniamhruaraidh

Previous books of FICTION by the author are:

It's Too Late To Die Young Now

Abbey

The Girl From Tir-na-nOg

The Confluence

Niamh

Friends

1

"HE'S SITTING OVER THERE BY THE LAKE. Good luck!"

"What does that mean? Good Luck."

"You'll find out . . . and you'll need it."

Edward was at Arbor Acres Retirement Village to meet with an elderly man and provide an hour or so of friendship and companionship through the auspices of his church and the outreach program they had created. Edward had volunteered one hour of his week to meet with an elderly person, usually someone who was alone, and provide this person with an opportunity to talk, complain, reminisce, or generally just converse with another human being. Most of the people living here who were alone were really alone, and any type of communication was helpful and appreciated.

Arbor Acres was a high-end retirement village. All its residents could afford the upscale retirement living it offered. All of the residents were financially set and successful economically; however, most of them were lonely, neglected, and frightened of what life lay ahead of them. Edward had met two ladies previously and each one had a different life, but basically, the same story.

The first lady was from Mt. Airy and had known Andy Griffith's family back in the day. Now, her family was scattered across the country, her husband had died earlier, and she was basically alone, except for some phone calls at Christmas and Mother's Day. The second lady he met had family in Winston-Salem, where Edward lived and Arbor Acres was located, but her family basically ignored her. It wasn't easy growing old. It saddened Edward to hear the stories of neglect and apathy. He was not really looking forward to his meeting this afternoon with the old man he'd been assigned to on this visit.

Edward worked at Goodwill Industries, was on the board at his Moravian church, and he had a good heart. A lonely heart, but a good one. Edward was thirty-seven years old and had been divorced from the only woman he'd ever dated before his marriage, or after his marriage. That was eleven years ago. His ex-wife told him she needed "more adventure" in her life, and promptly ran off with a guy who rode a BMW motorcycle—he didn't even have a car. Edward always thought he'd marry again and have a family . . . but he didn't. He always thought he'd be happy . . . but he wasn't. And he always thought his wife would come back to him . . . she hasn't, and she won't. So here he is meeting with people as lonely as he is, each one trying to fill a void in their lives that seems unfillable.

Edward looked out to the small lake where the attendant had pointed and saw several older people sitting on benches. He asked the attendant which one was Mr. Cleveland, the gentleman he's supposed to meet today. The attendant, who was busy helping an older lady into her wheelchair, replied, "He's the one on the bench, left of the middle."

Edward walked down the path towards the old guy and noticed a cane leaning against his leg and a book lying on the bench, with a yellow marker on top of it. It seemed as though the old guy might be asleep so Edward stood off to the side wondering if he should wake him up or not. Suddenly, the man exclaimed, "Are you going to sit down or not?"

"Yes, sir. Thank you. My name's Edward . . ." But before could finish, the old guy said,

"I know who you are. You don't have to stay. You can leave anytime. It's fine with me."

Edward nodded and tried to gather himself a little. Most older people love the attention and welcome someone to talk with. Apparently, Mr. Cleveland wasn't like most older people. Edward said, "No, sir. I'm fine. I'll stay awhile if you don't mind. It's a beautiful day and the lake is very relaxing." Then Edward continued, "I'm with the Moravian church, Mr. Cleveland . . ." At that point, he was interrupted again.

"If you're going to stay here, then call me, 'Dink.' It's what all my friends used to call me. Mr. Cleveland is too formal and has too many syllables. Just call me, Dink."

"Okay, Dink, you can call me Edward."

"I'll call you Ed. Fewer syllables and easier to say."

Edward nodded at him and continued, "I'd really prefer to be called Edward, that's what my parents named me and it's what everyone else knows me by."

Dink turned to look directly at him and said, "Okay, Ed . . . what did you want to talk about today?"

"Anything at all, Dink. Whatever is on your mind. Do you want to tell me about your family?"

Dink immediately said, "Okay, Ed, we'll talk about cancer."

"Cancer? Why do you want to talk about that?"

"Because I'm eaten up with cancer. I don't have long to educate you, Ed. I can't be wasting time on trivial matters."

Edward didn't quite know how to respond to that. He didn't know anything about Dink's personal life or medical history. He could tell Dink had something wrong with him though. His right arm was limp and his right hand was formed into a fist that never seemed to open. Dink noticed him looking at his right hand and volunteered, "I had a stroke when I was younger than you. Paralyzed me on my right side. My right leg and arm are virtually useless. But at the same time, the stroke did something to my brain which, no one believes but me, but it made it stronger or increased the capacity somehow. And for some reason, I remember everything I read or hear. Ever since the stroke, I've been crippled, but also became more intelligent and more inquisitive."

Edward didn't know how to respond, so he just nodded, and Dink continued, "I never had to work because my parents took care of me financially—they were rich. I started investing with the money they left me and now I'm extremely rich. I don't even know how to spend it all, Ed. But, unfortunately, all the money in the world cannot buy a cure for cancer. But I'm not going to sit here and cry about my condition. My goal is to enlighten someone and teach them things . . . looks like you're elected, Ed."

Edward didn't know what to say. He kept nodding, then finally asked, "Have you tried enlightening some of the other residents here?"

"Ed, take a look around. What do you see? A bunch of old people who are only concerned with what's for dinner, what kind of wine to drink, and when the next nap is. None of that is bad, but they just don't care anymore about the world or anything that happens in it. They're not inquisitive, they're not hungry for knowledge . . . they only want to enjoy their lives, eating and drinking and napping. I don't blame them. But I'm not like that! If that bothers you, then you need to get up and leave—or else we're going to discuss cancer. Up to you, Ed."

2

EDWARD DIDN'T LEAVE.

Dink started talking as he gazed out into the small lake. Never once did he falter or hesitate with any of his facts. "Ed, over 20,000 people die of cancer every day." He let that fact sink in, then continued, "Cancer causes more deaths than AIDS, tuberculosis, and malaria combined. Half of all the men in our country will contract cancer in their lifetime. That's the bad news, Ed. The good news is that about a third of all cancer could be prevented by avoiding tobacco and alcohol, having a healthy diet, and physical activity. Even something as simple as walking can reduce breast cancer by 25%! But will people walk?"

Edward didn't respond, he didn't know how to respond. Dink continued, "Sometimes people are just crazy. There are more skin cancer cases due to indoor tanning than lung cancer cases due to smoking—that's just crazy!" At this point, he looked over at Edward to make sure he had his attention, then continued, "Some of the residents living here are helping themselves without even knowing it—red wine kills cancer cells—but I doubt they know that. And, there are dogs who can sniff out prostate cancer with 98% accuracy—if we'd only use them."

Dink was quiet for a moment and Edward started to ask a question, then thought better of it. They both stared at the lake for a few moments before Dink said, "I'm going to die soon, Ed. I'm not afraid of it, death gets us all eventually. I read once that 153,000 people die every year on their birthday. Not much of a present is it? And doctors?? Did you know that over 7,000 people will die this year because of a doctor's sloppy handwriting, where nurses couldn't understand what he meant?"

Edward was too stunned to answer.

"Ed, did you know that more people commit suicide in New York City than are murdered there? And nationally, someone commits suicide every forty seconds—every forty seconds, Ed . . . that's so sad. One person is killed every hour in the U.S. by a drunk driver. And six hundred Americans die every year just from falling out of bed—falling out of bed, Ed!"

"How do you know all this stuff, Dink? I mean, that's a lot of statistics to memorize."

"I don't memorize them, Ed. I read a lot and remember things . . . like I told you. You can too if you put your mind to it. Did you know that malaria is thought to be responsible for the deaths of about half of the people who ever lived? Yet, road accidents now kill more people around the world than malaria. And here I am with all this money and yet over 20,000 children die worldwide every day due to poverty."

"You're starting to scare me, Dink. I was going to the beach soon, but with all this talk about death, now I'm afraid a shark might eat me." Edward's attempt at humor missed the mark.

"Ed, sharks kill 12 people a year worldwide, that's all. You are more likely to be killed by a falling coconut than from a shark attack. Heck, vending machines kill 13 people a year! We're all going to die, Ed, we just don't know how. You could die like I am by letting cancer eat you up, or you could die like the Greek philosopher Chrysippus, who is said to have died of laughter after getting his donkey drunk while trying to eat figs!"

Ed laughed at that. Dink didn't.

They each sat there staring out across the lake. Dink was thinking. Edward was thinking, "What now?"

"Ed, don't be like me. Spend your money on experiences, not on possessions . . . you'll be happier." Edward nodded but didn't say anything, so Dink continued, "You know, Ed, Americans spend over $15 billion a year on blue jeans. Think of that. Reduce world hunger or buy blue jeans. Do you own blue jeans, Ed?"

"Well, yeah, I do."

"Do you have money in the bank? Not being nosy, but I'm gonna die soon."

"I have some. Not a lot, like you. But some."

"Ed, if you have $10 in the bank and no debts, you are wealthier than 25% of all Americans. That's a sad statistic of our country."

Edward nodded and added, "Well, we can't all be like Bill Gates."

Dink suddenly turned his entire body towards Edward and asked, "Do you actually know how much money Bill Gates has, Ed?" Before Edward could answer, "No." Dink said, "If he spent a million dollars a day—every day—it would take him 218 years to spend all his money!"

Edward sighed, "Wow."

Then Dink continued, "The company, Apple, earns $300,000 per minute, Ed. Think about that!"

"How do people get so much money? It's hard to understand, Dink."

"A lot of them are like me, they inherited it. 19 of the 20 richest women in the country all inherited their money from either their husband or their father. Some of the men got theirs illegally, like that drug lord down in South America, Pablo Escobar. He had so much cash that rats ate almost one billion dollars of his money each year."

Edward said, "Well, the average American, like me, will never have to worry about rats eating our money."

"Right, because the average American spends over a third of his income on interest from credit cards and car loans. They're making the credit card companies rich instead of themselves! Then they get home and argue about money, or the lack thereof, which is ultimately the top predictor of divorce in our country! Plus, Americans spend more money on their pets each year than Germany does on its entire defense budget. I'm boring you, aren't I, Ed? Sometimes I get wound up and don't know when to stop."

"No, I'm fascinated that you know all this stuff. I was going to go home and check some of your facts, but I can't even remember half of them."

"You don't need to check them . . . they're all true." Then Dink looked over at Ed and asked him, "Are you married?"

"No, sir. Been divorced over eleven years."

"Did your wife have big boobs, Ed?"

"What? Big boobs? Why do you want to know that?"

"Just curious, Ed, I read a study once that found that men who prefer large breasts are less financially secure."

Edward didn't know if he should be insulted, or get mad, or simply laugh at Dink's statement. He looked over at Dink and replied, "Money is not the reasoning behind everything, Dink. Sometimes it can be just love, or maybe even just sex and not about money."

Dink looked back out at the lake and said, "Really? I read a report several years ago about a psychologist and an economist who taught a group of monkeys the concept of money. Soon, the monkeys engaged in prostitution. Believe me, Ed, it's all about the money."

After a few silent moments, Dink told Ed, "I'd better be getting back inside; today is wine and cheese at the meeting hall . . . I don't want to miss that."

"Okay, Dink, let me give you a hand."

"I don't need any help! Sorry, Ed, but I'm fine."

To be paralyzed on his entire right side, Dink seemed to walk pretty well. Ed walked beside him, in silence, on the way back to the buildings. Suddenly, Dink stopped and bent over and picked up a penny he saw lying on the sidewalk. He put the penny in his pocket, then looked at Edward and said, "Americans throw away $62 million worth of coins every year . . . not me! I'll pick up pennies all day, but I won't touch a dollar bill."

Edward bit on that comment, "Why not?"

"Because, Ed, paper money can transport live flu virus for over two weeks! And, an average dollar bill has been found to have vaginal bacteria, microbes from mouths, DNA from pets and viruses. No, sir! No dollar bills for me."

When they reached the door, Edward opened it for Dink, who then said, "I have two questions for you, Ed."

"Okay, ask away."

"First, did you know that if you would spin a penny on a table, that it would land on tails 80% of the time?"

Edward smiled and replied, "No, I didn't know that. But it might come in handy one day. What's your other question?"

"Are you coming back to visit me?"

"Yeah, I'll be back."

And with that, Edward shook Dink's left hand, they smiled at each other and Dink went in to have a glass of red wine and a plate of cheese. Edward just went home.

3

EDWARD WENT TO WORK. He went to church. He shopped for groceries. He called his mom and dad. He watched television. But mostly, he thought about Dink. He thought about his cancer and his paralyzed right leg and arm and how he could remember all those statistics he threw out so easily. Edward could only remember a few of them, which he checked, and true to Dink's word—they were all correct.

He wasn't supposed to go visit Arbor Acres but once every two weeks, but he called ahead to inquire if he could come back after only one week. He was told the older lady from Mt. Airy would love to see him again. No . . . he lied and told them he had something he had to return to Mr. Cleveland and needed to see him if that was possible. It was.

When he parked his car, he saw Dink sitting on the same bench, near the lake, left of the middle. When he walked up to the bench, Dink immediately said, "I hope I didn't bore you too much last week, talking about cancer and death and such." Before Edward could answer, Dink continued, "Sit down and let me tell you about something less macabre. Have you ever heard of Marilyn Monroe, Ed? I know you have—everybody has. But let me really tell you about her."

Edward sat down without saying a word and Dink began his story, "As a child, she was in and out of foster homes. She lived in an orphanage and had eleven sets of foster parents after her mother was institutionalized in a psychiatric facility. She never knew her father and was living with a family friend when this family decided to move to West Virginia, leaving her behind. Unless she got married, she'd be turned back over to an orphanage. The family knew a twenty-year-old guy next door and suggested they marry. So, eighteen days later, just after she turned 16 years old—they married.

She eventually made it out to Hollywood and soon posed for a new magazine called "Playboy." She was paid $50 for those initial pictures which graced the first edition of "Playboy." That edition made Hugh Hefner millions of dollars. All Marilyn ever got was the lousy fifty bucks.

All through her acting career, she was taken advantage of. She was often paid less than her colleagues, despite her super famous status or how much the public loved her. In one of her more famous roles in "Gentlemen Prefer Blondes," her colleague Jane Russel was paid about ten times more than Marilyn was. In her last move, with Dean Martin, he was paid five times more than her. She was always making money for other people, rather than for herself. Even the dress she wore when she so famously sang "Happy Birthday" to President Kennedy in 1962, set a world record for the most expensive piece of clothing ever sold, at $1,267,500." Dink glanced over at Ed to see if he was paying attention . . . he was.

"She most famously married the baseball star Joe DiMaggio, but it lasted only 274 days. Joe blew up and got mad when he saw her filming the famous scene where her skirt billows up over a subway grate. It was shot in front of a large crowd and DiMaggio got flustered that everyone was seeing his wife's legs and underwear. They fought over it and soon the two separated and Marilyn filed for divorce on the grounds of 'mental cruelty.'

But DiMaggio continued to be there when she needed him. Joe even thought that shortly before her death, they would get remarried. When she died, he was in charge of the funeral—and refused to let anyone from Hollywood attend the service. He said, 'Tell them, if it wasn't for them, she'd still be here.' Then, he had roses delivered to her grave twice a week for 20 years.

She was buried in the crypt below the one DiMaggio bought for himself, but he sold it years later. Hugh Hefner bought the plot next to hers, but even though he made millions from her pictures, the two never actually met each other."

When it seemed as though Dink had finished his story of Marilyn Monroe, Edward asked, "How did she die, Dink? I remember there were questions about it."

"Well, she had been in deteriorating health for a few years and was seeing a psychiatrist at the time. She complained of insomnia and started getting addicted to prescription drugs. Those drugs and then alcohol began to take a toll on her health. She was found dead in her bed in 1962 at her home there in Brentwood. She was only 36 years old . . . what a shame. The cause of her death was officially ruled as "probable suicide" due to acute barbiturate poisoning. But Ed . . . there are a lot of people that still think the Kennedy's had something to do with it. She was smitten with JFK and had dreams of being the First Lady one day. But everybody knew that would never happen."

Edward and Dink sat gazing out at the lake, thinking about Marilyn; each to his own intuition. Then Dink asked, "Ed, why did you get divorced?"

It took Edward a few moments to decide if he wanted to discuss that, but he eventually answered, "I didn't divorce her, Dink; she divorced me."

"Why?"

"Said she wanted more life in her life."

For once, Dink didn't have anything to add. They watched six or seven geese come floating in over the trees and land in the lake. Then Dink said, "Did you know that ducks sleep with one eye opened so they can watch for predators?"

Edward responded, "Those aren't ducks. They're geese."

Dink wasn't fazed, "And most parrots usually learn about 50 words, but there's one in a zoo in Tennessee that can say over 200 words."

Edward smiled and added, "I bet his first words were, "Why am I in Tennessee and how do I get out."

For the first time in their brief friendship, Edward saw a slight smile on Dink's face.

"But sometimes, captive ravens can talk more than parrots! And ostriches have the largest eyes of any animal that lives on land. It's about the size of a billiard ball—their eyes are actually bigger than their brains."

Edward added, "I've known a few women like that." And Dink smiled again.

"Were you ever married, Dink?"

For once, it seemed as though Dink might be left speechless. But then, "No. Who would want to marry an old cripple like me?"

"Well, you weren't always crippled were you?"

Again, Dink was silent and Edward left him to his thoughts. Then he answered, "I had a girlfriend once, in fact, we were engaged. But then I had the stroke and everything changed. She stayed with me for a while during my recovery, but I knew it wouldn't last. I couldn't expect a smart, beautiful girl like that to stick with a cripple . . . it wouldn't have been fair to her."

"So she left you because of the stroke?"

"No! I ran her off. Told her to go have a life. She didn't want to, but I stopped allowing her to come around. I had to. It was for her own good."

After a few moments of silence, Edward finally said, "We're a fine pair aren't we Dink? You run your woman off and my woman runs off."

Dink closed his eyes and solemnly replied, "Could've been worse . . . they could've stayed."

4

EDWARD NOW HAD A STANDING APPOINTMENT each week with Dink. The leadership at the church was thrilled he was taking an active role. Arbor Acres was thrilled he was volunteering his time to help with the life experience of one of their residents. And for once in his life, Edward was thrilled with something, anything.

The following week, after he parked his car, he looked out at the lake and didn't see Dink anywhere. He walked inside and the receptionist told him Dink had a doctor's appointment but was due back anytime. She offered him some coffee and seemed very friendly. Edward asked her questions about Arbor Acres and about her role, then he asked if she knew Mr. Cleveland very well.

"Nobody knows Mr. Cleveland very well. He's not as sociable as some of our other residents." Edward asked her what she meant. She said, "Well, most people try to get along . . . you know, 'When in Rome.' But, with Mr. Cleveland, it's 'When in Rome, they do as HE does.'"

Edward replied, "Yeah, I can see that . . . sort of."

She added, "Time waits on no one . . . but him. When he walks down the sidewalk, the roses stop to smell him. That's Mr. Cleveland."

At this point, Edward was trying to find a graceful escape route out of the reception area. Fortunately, he looked outside and saw the male attendant he met before and waved to him as though he were his friend. He excused himself from the receptionist and walked outside. The attendant, whose name was Johnny, told him Mr. Cleveland would be back shortly, the van was expected any moment. Edward said, "Thanks, Mr. Cleveland seems to have quite the reputation around here."

Johnny answered, "Yes, sir, he's definitely a character alright. He lives vicariously through himself."

Edward asked, "Is he difficult, Johnny? Are people here afraid of him?"

Johnny smiled and added, "You know how some people are afraid of the dark? Well, the dark is afraid of him."

"Does he have many friends here?"

"Mr. Cleveland? Have friends? Let's just say he's unique . . . and leave it at that."

Edward was intrigued now and asked what he meant by that. Johnny smiled at him and replied, "You know when a tree falls in the forest and no one is there to hear it? He hears it!"

Just then they both saw the van pulling around the corner towards them. They waited until the door opened and they saw Mr. Cleveland making his way towards the steps. However, before he exited the van he stopped and looked at the driver of the van and said, "No, I don't have a cell phone. And I'll tell you why . . . the average person unlocks their smartphone 110 times a day—wasted time! And did you know that more people have died taking selfies last year than by shark attacks—it's true. Apple sold 340,000 iPhones every day last year, and you know why they sold so many?"

The driver was still staring out the window, but answered, "No, sir, I don't."

"Because in Britain, every year, 100,000 phones are dropped down the toilet. That's how stupid humans are. More Africans have access to cell phone service than piped water and electricity. In fact, in the entire world, more people have cell phones than have toilets! And the worst statistic of all: 9% of Americans admit using their cell phones during sex! What is the world coming to . . . I'm sorry, I forgot your name."

"It's Russ, sir. I hope you have a nice day." Russ and Johnny and all the other employees at Arbor Acres know they just have to grin and bear it at times. Old people have their ways . . . and then, there's Mr. Cleveland!

Johnny tried to help Mr. Cleveland down the steps of the van, but Dink waved him away. Johnny turned to leave and caught the eye of Edward and said, "Good luck."

Dink looked at Edward and said, "Let's go inside and have a glass of wine." He didn't ask Edward if wanted a glass a wine, or if he even drank wine—that didn't matter. They found two chairs near the corner and settled in while they waited for the server to come over.

"How did your doctor's visit go? Is everything alright?"

"No, it's not alright, Ed. I'm dying. I told you that! Why don't you go up there and bring us a glass of wine back so we don't have to wait on the server."

"Okay. What kind do you like?"

"The kind made with grapes. Quit dawdling and hurry up!"

Edward went to the serving area and ordered two glasses of Chardonnay. He didn't know a lot about wine, but he'd heard of Chardonnay before. The wine steward asked, "Is this for Mr. Cleveland?"

Edward answered, "Yes, does he not like this kind of wine?"

"Oh, Mr. Cleveland likes all kinds of wine. We all respect his wishes and his comments."

Edward smiled and said, "I totally understand. He certainly demands respect."

The wine steward handed the two glasses over and replied, "The mosquitoes around here refuse to bite him purely out of respect." Edward believed it.

As soon as Edward sat down with the wine, Dink began, "Ed, did you know that when Columbus 'discovered' the Americas, the continent was already inhabited by 90 million people? Which was a third of the world's population at that time! And also, there are more people in slavery today than at any time in human history." He looked over at Edward to make sure he was paying attention. Edward was, and he nodded attentively, then asked,

"Dink, what sort of cancer do you have?"

"Dink looked him fiercely in the eyes and said, "Over the past 3,400 years, humans have been entirely at peace for only 268 of them or just 8% of recorded history. That should tell you all you need to know about human beings, Ed."

"Is it lung cancer, Dink?"

"And another thing, the pyramids were built by paid laborers, Ed. Not slaves, that was a myth perpetuated by the Greeks.

"Couldn't be brain cancer, could it?"

"And did you know that the life expectancy in ancient Rome was only twenty to thirty years, Ed? And people always think the Roman Empire was so mighty, I'll have you know that it was only the 28th largest empire in history—the 28th!"

"Liver cancer?"

"I'll tell you what's sad, Ed . . . humans are 50% heavier in the last hundred years than they have been throughout most of human history. And speaking of human history, in the last five thousand years only one disease has been eradicated—and it isn't cancer—smallpox . . . that's the only one."

"Melanoma?"

"Ed, we are now living in the most peaceful time in human history. And speaking of human history, are you aware that only once—once, Ed, has a submarine sunk another submerged submarine? Only once."

Edward looked over at Dink and said again, "You know my name's Edward . . . right?"

Dink took a small sip of his wine, set the glass down and said, "Stomach cancer, Ed. That's what's killing me."

"Well, what do the doctor's say about it, Dink?"

"They say I'm going to die, Ed. Haven't you been paying attention to anything I've been telling you?"

Edward smiled and thought this would be a good time to surprise Dink. Last night as he was eating a pork chop sandwich from a food truck near downtown, it reminded him of how much he liked bacon and ham and basically anything from a pig. So when he got home, he googled pigs to find some information that might impress Dink.

"Dink, did you know that a pig can drink up to fourteen gallons of water a day? And that one time, a mother pig had 37 piglets, of which 36 were born alive . . . and 33 of them survived!" He looked over at Dink to see his reaction, there was none, so he continued, "There was a pig born in China one time that eventually weighed 2,552 pounds and was five feet tall and nine feet long!" Still nothing from Dink. "And pigs are extremely intelligent. They're thought to be as smart as a three year old human and smarter than most dogs and monkeys."

Edward took a small sip of wine to give Dink the opportunity to comment, but he was still quiet. So he continued, "And, Dink, there is only one pig in all of

Afghanistan, and it lives in the Kabul zoo. Whereas in Denmark, there are twice as many pigs as people!" Still nothing. "Finally, FDR himself once said that 'Dogs look up to man. Cats look down to man. But pigs look us straight in the eye and see an equal.'"

Edward was extremely proud of himself for remembering all those facts. He had studied them all evening, just for this moment. He took another congratulatory sip of wine and noticed Dink turn towards him, probably to congratulate him, but no . . . Dink said, "It wasn't FDR who said that it was Churchill."

5

EDWARD HAD INCREASED HIS VISITS to Dink to twice a week now. He could also tell Dink didn't have the stamina he had a few weeks ago. Whether it was old age, though Edward didn't know exactly how old Dink was, or cancer, or both— but he was visibly weaker. Not his mind—just his frail, crippled body. Edward tried in vain to get more personal information from Dink but was always unsuccessful. He even tried coaxing information from the staff at Arbor Acres . . . they would not divulge any personal information at all.

He did find an older, wheelchair-bound gentleman at Arbor Acres who seemed to have been acquaintances with Dink in the past. His name was Mr. Ruby. Apparently Mr. Ruby and Dink had a friendship several years ago that had disintegrated due to Dink's overbearing personality. Understandable. Edward set up a meeting with Mr. Ruby in his cottage one afternoon, after Mr. Ruby's nap. When the initial pleasantries were exchanged, Edward told him why he wanted to meet with him: to find out something about Dink.

Mr. Ruby nodded, then rubbed his bald head and said, "He's a mean-spirited, lonesome, know-it-all, who thinks everyone else is either stupid or incompetent. Other than that, I like him just fine. We used to play cards together, but I always suspected him of cheating, because he always won. I mean he ALWAYS won—he never lost. Now, that's just not possible, which you know if you've ever played cards. So, one day, after I lost again, I accused him of cheating. He got mad and huffed off and we haven't spoken since."

Edward asked, "Do you know anything about his personal life or history?"

"Not much. I know he's well off and doesn't have any financial worries. But he never talked about any family and never answered any questions about his career. I never knew what he did. He's a strange man. Always spouting off facts and statistics that nobody in the world cared about. I don't know how he came up with all that nonsense."

Edward and Mr. Ruby talked a while longer, but more about Mr. Ruby and his family and children and grandchildren. Nothing else about Dink. After about forty-five minutes, Mr. Ruby told Edward he needed to get to physical therapy, so their meeting ended with Edward not really knowing any more than he knew beforehand.

Edward walked back outside and found Dink, sitting out by the lake again, contemplating nature, or whatever it is that an old man who is dying contemplates. Edward sat on the bench and asked Dink what he was thinking about. He didn't really expect an answer, but he got one. "I'm thinking about my friend, John Fairfax. I miss him. He was probably the only human being I could stand to be around who didn't bore me to death."

This news that Dink had a friend shocked Edward. "Did this Mr. Fairfax live here at Arbor Acres?"

"No. He'd never live here. This place could never hold him."

"Where does he live now? Anywhere close? Maybe you could visit him."

"He's dead. He was living out near Las Vegas and had a heart attack, they say. Not sure I believe it, but that's what they say."

Edward was a little confused, "He was living in Las Vegas when he died, and he was your friend? Did you live in Vegas before?"

"No." Dink said, "I met him in London back in the 60's. We were both living there at the time."

"You lived in London in the 1960's?"

"Focus, Ed. I can't keep repeating everything. I'm trying to tell you about my friend, now pay attention. I met John in London and then we kept in contact and visited when he lived in the states from time to time. He moved around a lot. He wasn't the sort of guy to be stuck in one place. That all started in his childhood. He was born, an only child, in Rome to an English father and a Bulgarian mother. He barely knew his father and soon took a keen interest in the outdoors and nature. He joined the scouts and on a camping trip when he was nine years old, he got into a fight and settled it by stealing the scoutmaster's gun and settling the dispute quickly.

He got kicked out of the scouts, of course, and moved to Buenos Aires when he was thirteen years old and soon ran away and moved into the jungle and supported himself by hunting jaguars and ocelots and selling their hides. Then he became a pirate for a few years, where he learned about the sea and boats. John was the kind of man that if he were to say something costs an arm and a leg . . . it would.

After this is when I met him in London when he was at loose ends. His days as a pirate had lit a fire in him though and the thought came into his mind that he wanted to row a boat across the Atlantic Ocean and then the Pacific Ocean."

Edward interrupted and asked, "He wanted to row a boat across the ocean?"

"Yes, Ed, am I not speaking clearly? He would practice his rowing on the lake at Hyde Park—hour after hour he spent rowing. Back and forth, back and forth."

Edward interrupted again and asked, "But I don't understand why he wanted to row a boat across the ocean."

"Because it was there, Ed! Don't you get it?"

"Oh."

"Now, if I can continue . . . In 1969 he pushed off in January from the Canary Islands, bound for Florida. His rowboat, which he named Britannia, was 22 feet long and made of mahogany. It had been created for the voyage as a self-righting, self-bailing vessel. All he carried with him were spam, oatmeal, brandy, water, and a temperamental radio. There was no support boat and no chase plane like those wimps today use, it was only John and the sea. Sometimes he said he caught some fish and a few times he spotted some passing ships and they gave him some food and water.

The long, empty days spawned a temporary madness in him. He started talking to the planet Venus as he longed for female companionship. He once told me that he honestly thought Venus was talking back to him." At this point in the story, Dink drifted off to far-away thoughts. Edward was smart enough to let those thoughts assimilate and return of their own accord.

Dink continued, "In July of that year, after 180 days at sea—alone—all tanned, tired, and about twenty pounds lighter, he made landfall at Hollywood, Florida. After medical attention, his first words to the press were, 'This is bloody stupid.' Two years later he was at it again."

Edward asked, "He rowed across the Atlantic again?"

"No, Ed. The Pacific. Pay attention! John had met a young lady when he was doing his rowing training in London, named Ms. Cook, and he somehow convinced her to go along with him across the Pacific. John could talk anybody into anything . . . he was something else. Anyway, he and Ms. Cook stocked their little 36-foot long rowboat and took off from San Francisco to cross the Pacific.

John told me the Pacific was much rougher than the Atlantic. They had a rudder that got snapped clean off in a storm and were frequently swamped and turned around. John was bitten on the arm by a shark during the voyage and they ran into a cyclone, where they had to lash themselves to the boat so they wouldn't get thrown overboard.

For a while, they were presumed lost and dead. Finally, after 361 days at sea, and after rowing over 8,000 miles, they landed in Australia. John was asked why he didn't sail across the ocean instead of row. He said, 'Anybody with a little bit of knowledge can sail. I'm after a battle with nature, primitive and raw.' I've never forgotten that quote of his . . . I wish I could've gone with him.

He finally settled into a life of gambling playing baccarat. He was very good at it and I would occasionally join him for games in Vegas or Europe, but I was just in it for the fun and to listen to John talk. Boy, did he ever have some stories . . ."

Edward was smart enough not to interrupt at this point, even though it was apparent the story was over. He gave Dink time to think and reminisce about John Fairfax— hunter, pirate, explorer, adventurer, gambler, and friend.

6

EDWARD WAS INTRIGUED that Dink had spent time in Las Vegas, so he asked him about it. Normally, Dink never answered any direct, personal questions about his life, but he seemed eager to tell Edward what he knew about Las Vegas. And he knew a lot.

"Ed, people are confused about Las Vegas—just like you are. Contrary to popular belief, prostitution is not legal there. You see, the law in Nevada only permits prostitution in counties with a population of fewer than 400,000 people. Obviously, Vegas has a lot more people than that. Reno is the same way, no prostitution there either.

Ed, it would take 288 years for one person to spend one night in every hotel room in Las Vegas . . . did you know that?" Of course, Edward did not know that, so he didn't answer. "And 15 of the world's top 25 hotels are located in Las Vegas. They did a study once that showed that 15% of people come to Las Vegas primarily to gamble, however, 71% actually do gamble. If you wanted to buy an acre of prime land on 'The Strip' it would cost you between three and six million dollars."

Edward broke in and asked, "Did you do a lot of gambling out there, Dink?"

"You don't have to go to Las Vegas to gamble, Ed, today there are forms of legalized gambling in 48 of the 50 states. People go there now, not to gamble, but to get married. The average number of weddings each day in Vegas is 315. They make it easy, the cost of a marriage license in Nevada is only $35, whereas the cost of filing for divorce is $450. And, Ed, did you know that when astronauts look at the earth from outer space that the Las Vegas Strip is the brightest spot on earth?"

"No, I didn't know that."

"I'm sure you didn't. Just like you didn't know that FedEx was saved from closing back in its early days by Las Vegas."

"What?" Edward had no idea where this was going.

"The founder and CEO of FedEx saved his company by gambling in Vegas. He took FedEx's last $5,000 there and won $27,000 gambling on blackjack, which paid for the company's $24,000 fuel bill. Without winning that money, FedEx would have closed the doors, Ed. But not all the gambling is good in Vegas. One year, a Las Vegas hospital had to suspend workers who were betting on when patients would die. One nurse was even accused of murdering a patient so she would win. And over a third of all thefts and cheating incidents from casinos are committed by people on their own staffs.

Ed, there's a reason why Las Vegas has a higher number of unlisted phone numbers than any other city in the United States. Gambling! One time a man bet $100 in a slot machine and won $39 million. And there was another man, named Archie Karas, who took $50 to Vegas and turned it into $40 million, then promptly lost it all. That's the nature of Las Vegas, Ed. Don't you be going there!"

"But you went there, Dink."

"I went there to visit my friend, John Fairfax, and to do some research—not to gamble."

Edward exclaimed, "Research? Really, Dink?"

"Yes, Ed, did you know that Las Vegas only gets about four inches of rain a year? And, that shrimp consumption in Vegas is over 60,000 pounds per day! That's higher than the rest of the nation combined. Think about that, Ed. More than forty-one million people visit there every year and there are over 22,000 conventions held there every year. Ed . . . the average person loses almost $600 every time they visit Vegas. Do the math."

Edward was overwhelmed. It must've taken a lot out of Dink as well, who then said, "Ed, I'm going to lay down. Come back tomorrow if you can." And with that, Dink picked up his cane and shuffled back to his place. Edward watched him leave, but continued to sit and contemplate the lake, the geese, John Fairfax, and Las Vegas . . . it was a lot to think about.

———————◦———————

Edward went back over to Arbor Acres on Monday and found Dink inside sipping a cup of hot chocolate. Dink invited him to sit and told him he wasn't feeling very well, his stomach was bothering him. Edward understood. They both sat there and Dink was unusually quiet. He finally looked over at Edward and said, "Go ahead, I know you want to ask me something."

Edward didn't really have anything in mind, but he took this opportunity to ask something that he'd always wondered about. "Okay, what's your real first name? It's not 'Dink' is it? If not, where did 'Dink' come from?"

"I don't like that question, ask another one."

"Okay." Edward thought a moment then asked, "Tell me about your family. Your mom and dad and anybody else close to you."

It seemed as though Dink took a long, deep breath . . . then said, "That's not important. Ask a relevant question."

Edward knew full well that Dink would not answer this next question, but he asked it anyway, "Tell me about your fiancé, what was she like? How long did you know her?"

Much to Edward's surprise, Dink began, "She was left-handed. And right-handed. Her passport required no photograph. She could speak Russian . . . in French. Her pillow was cool on BOTH sides. She never walked into a spider web. Cars would look both ways for her, before driving down the street." He stopped briefly and Edward thought he saw moisture in Dink's eyes, then Dink said, "Panhandlers gave her money. And she never wore a watch because time was always on her side."

Edward was stunned. He'd never heard such a description before. He couldn't fathom how to ask another question after hearing that answer. Dink sat there and let his hot chocolate go cold, he didn't seem to care.

———————◦———————

Each man sat for a while, each one lost in his own thoughts. Then, Dink suddenly spoke up, "Do you remember Mt. St. Helen's, Ed?" Before Edward could actually answer, Dink continued, "Back in 1980, scientists kept monitoring the mountain, watching as a bulge on the north side kept getting bigger and bigger. It finally erupted and a 250-foot wide vent opened up and ash blasted out at 650 miles per hour, 10,000 feet up in the air. The ash itself caused static electricity and lightning bolts.

Ash, rocks, gas, and glacial ice roared down the side of the mountain at 100 miles per hour. It buried the local river in 150 feet of debris for fourteen miles. Magma, at 1,300 degrees Fahrenheit, flowed for miles. It demolished a 230-square mile area around the mountain. The local geologist was on his radio to the main office when he heard the explosion. He was only able to say, 'Vancouver, Vancouver, this is it!' before he was killed by the blast. Millions of trees, millions, Ed, were scorched and burned by the hot air alone.

When the glacier atop the mountain melted, a massive mudslide wiped out homes and dammed up rivers throughout the area. The plume of smoke and ash was carried by the wind as far away as Minnesota.

The falling ash clogged carburetors and thousands of motorists were stranded. Fifty-seven people died from suffocation, burns, and other assorted injuries. Only twenty-seven bodies were ever found. Mt. St. Helens went from 9,600 feet high to only 8,300 feet high in a matter of seconds."

Dink finished his story and each man was silent again. Although Edward had heard of Mt. St. Helens, he had never heard of it like Dink described it. After a few moments, Edward asked, "How do you know about all that?"

Dink looked over at him and quizzically replied, "How do you NOT know about it?"

7

DINK AND EDWARD HAD EVOLVED THEIR FRIENDSHIP into a relationship of needs . . . Dink needed Edward to talk to. He needed someone who would listen to him, someone who seemed to care. Whereas, Edward needed a mentor, someone to spend time with, someone to care about and listen to. They each fulfilled the needs of the other. And, their meetings were now happening on a nearly daily basis, which made them both happy, in an unspoken sort of way.

As Edward parked his car, he noticed Dink coming out of the building on his way to the bench by the lake. He started to offer his help, then thought better of it. He just ambled up beside Dink and they walked in silence to the bench and sat as they watched a lone, white swan floating on the far side. After a few minutes, Dink asked, "Why didn't you ever get married again?"

Edward didn't exactly know how to answer that question—at least truthfully. So he gave the old standby answer, "I guess I haven't found the right woman yet, Dink."

"Ed," Dink stated, "You see a lot of smart guys with dumb women, but you hardly ever see a smart woman with a dumb guy. And you know why that is, Ed?" Before Edward could actually answer that question, Dink continued, "Because while men may play the game, women know the score!"

Edward replied, "So you think women are smarter than us?"

"Ed, I don't think women are better than men, I think men are a lot worse than women." Edward looked confused. But Dink didn't give him time to think, he continued, "Even the wisest men make fools of themselves about women, Ed. And even the most foolish women are wise about men. A woman only needs to know one man well, in order to understand all men; whereas a man may know all women and understand not one of them.

Ed, here's all you need to know about men and women: women are crazy, men are stupid. And the main reason woman are crazy is that men are stupid. Face it, Ed, when we all get naked, women look better. Female bodies are beautiful, and nicer to look at than men. This is because a woman's body is designed like a sleek sports car; it has curves in the right places and the useful parts are tucked in the inside. A man's body is all screwed up. If it was a car, it would be considered both ugly and non-functional. They're all angular straight lines, have a boxy shape, and the gearshift is mounted on the front of the hood.

Aside from being naturally more beautiful, women know how to dress their bodies to look even better. A woman has all kinds of tricks to take care of things like puffy eyes and bad hair days. Men can barely figure out which T-shirt goes with a pair of jeans, and half the time whatever he chooses won't even fit correctly. Ed, you know who else can't dress themselves properly? Infants, old people on life support, and people with no arms!"

Dink showed no signs of letting up, so Edward remained quiet. "Ed, by using basic tools like short skirts, low-cut blouses, and lipstick, a woman can get all kinds of free stuff like drinks, food, admission to clubs, and cool gifts. And if that doesn't work, and she's in a real pinch, all she has to do is start crying. Crying makes everything go away and makes her boyfriend apologize for something he's not sure he ever did. This is a superpower and it can be used to manipulate the world around her."

Edward nodded in agreement; he wouldn't dare contradict Dink at this juncture. So Dink continued, "Ed, on average, women live longer than us. This suggests that women are stronger and healthier, and make better decisions than we do. And, women generally make better decisions about their diets, they drink less alcohol, and care about stuff like vitamins and doctor check-ups. A man won't do most of these things unless he's lucky enough to have a woman who tells him to do it.

You know, Ed, it takes one woman twenty years to make a man of her son—and another woman twenty minutes to make a fool of him. But there's a reason for all this . . . man was made at the end of the work week when God was tired."

After this, it seemed as though Dink was tired. He took a deep breath and Edward thought he was going to continue, but instead, he exhaled slowly and made a humming noise as he stared out at the lake. So Edward thought this was an opportunity to volunteer some personal information and get Dink's opinion. "I've been thinking about signing up with an online dating service, but haven't decided yet."

"I think it's a good idea. You know, Ed, in America today, about 42 million people have never been married, twice as many as in 1960. 23% of couples who meet through online dating sites, end up getting married. But be careful, Ed. There are some women out there who . . ."

Dink didn't finish that statement, so Edward asked, "Who what?"

"Just be careful, I read that 68% of women surveyed say they would have an affair if they could get away with it. And 1 in 3 women admit to regularly watching porn! Porn, Ed. Nowadays, 40% of all births in the U.S. come from unmarried women. Just be careful, Ed . . . be careful! A survey found that men spend almost a year of their lives staring at women. Whereas women spend nearly one year of their lives deciding what to wear. And, remember this, the average woman owns 19 pairs of shoes, but wears only 7."

Edward didn't know what that meant, or what relevance it had, but he nodded just the same.

Dink rose slowly from the bench and said, "Let's go have a glass of wine." As they were walking to the building, Dink kept stopping every few steps and Edward was worried something might be wrong with him.

"Are you okay?" He asked.

"Yeah, I'm just looking for pennies."

A few raindrops had started falling, so Dink cut his penny-looking short and they continued inside. Edward had a glass of Pinot Grigio and Dink had Merlot as they sat by a window and watched the rain intensify. After half a glass of quietness, Dink broke the silence, "A raindrop can fall as fast as 22 miles per hour, Ed. In some parts of the world, it can rain tadpoles and small fish. We get about 40 inches of rain a year here, but there's a place in Colombia that gets 534 inches of rain each year, Ed. That's a lot of rain! I think you should go ahead and sign up for that dating service. It'll do you good. You don't need to be hanging out so much with an old, crippled, dying man. Get out there, Ed . . . live a little."

Edward finished his wine, ate a small cheese square, rose from his seat, and said, "See you tomorrow, Dink. Thanks for the advice." As Edward walked out to his car, Dink sat thinking about a girl he once knew who didn't need a watch. About a girl who taught old dogs a variety of new tricks, and whose dress was never wrinkled . . . a girl who could kill two stones with one bird. A girl he could never forget. A girl he could only remember.

8

"ED, I WATCHED A PROGRAM on the science channel last night about the solar system. Tell me, how do they 'know' the sun is 4.6 billion years old? They've never been there, they can't measure it . . . how do they know?"

"I don't know, Dink. I guess the scientists have ways of checking those things."

"I know the sun is hot—I get it. But how do they know its 59 million degrees hot? It makes no sense. They said one million earths could fit inside the sun . . . that, I believe—they can measure the size."

Edward was aware enough to let Dink finish his rambling, which he did, "And they said the sun will continue to burn for another 130 million years! How do they know that, Ed? Seems to me like they make up this stuff and just expect us to believe it. I want to see the proof of how they arrived at those numbers. I need to get the address to that show and write to those people."

"Yeah, Dink. You should do that."

"Well, Ed, you can't just blindly believe everything you hear and what you see on television."

"I believe everything you tell me, Dink. Should I start checking your facts?"

"That's different, Ed, and you know it. I wouldn't ever lie to you. I always give you the straight facts . . . you know that!"

Edward nodded but didn't say anything. Dink looked at him very hard, but also didn't say anything. Then, Dink added, "Ed, let me tell you about Teddy Roosevelt. You know who he is don't you?"

"Yeah, Dink. I know who he is."

"Well tell me then. Exactly who is he?"

Edward thought a moment and said, "He was President of the United States in the early 1900's. He explored a lot out west and created several national parks. I think he even went to the Amazon once." Edward was proud of himself for knowing all that.

"Very good, Ed. But any seventh grader knows all that. Let me tell you something you don't know about him. He was campaigning for the presidency back in 1912, in Milwaukee, Wisconsin, when a man tried to assassinate him—did you know that?" Edward knew enough to simply shake his head 'no,' as Dink continued, " A man named Schrank had written that the ghost of William McKinley had told him to avenge his death. Of course, Roosevelt had nothing to do with William McKinley's death, but that's what this man, Schrank, wrote.

Schrank had followed Roosevelt from New Orleans all the way up to Milwaukee, waiting for his opportunity. When Teddy left his hotel there and went to his car, he stopped to acknowledge the cheering crowd—that's when Schrank acted. He pulled a gun and shot Roosevelt at point blank range, hitting him in the chest. Fortunately, the bullet also hit Roosevelt's steel eyeglass case and a fifty-page copy of his speech, which he was carrying in his pocket.

An aide tackled Schrank and wrestled him to the ground, taking away the gun. Roosevelt stumbled a little, but straightened himself, raised his hat, and smiled at the crowd. Another aide asked him if he was hit, but he only said, 'He pinked me, Harry.' Several people in the crowd began pummeling Schrank and others starting screaming to 'kill him.' Roosevelt saw what was happening and shouted to the crowd, 'Don't hurt him. Bring him here. I want to see him.' They brought Schrank face to face with Roosevelt and Teddy looked him squarely in the face to see if he recognized him. Seeing that he didn't know the man, Roosevelt asked him, 'What did you do it for?' Schrank didn't answer, so Roosevelt said, 'You poor creature.' And then told the police to make sure no harm came to him.

Roosevelt waved again to the crowd and took off in his car. Since he wasn't coughing up blood, he refused to go to the hospital, even though his shirt was bloody. He gave his speech, which lasted 90 minutes, then later went to the hospital for medical attention. An x-ray showed the bullet had lodged in his chest muscle and doctors concluded it would be safer to leave it where it was than to risk removing it. Roosevelt carried the bullet with him for the rest of his life.

Schrank was committed to a hospital for the criminally insane and remained there for 29 more years before he died in 1943 of pneumonia." Dink paused and looked over at Edward, who said,

"No. I didn't know that." Dink smiled.

When Edward arrived, the two men went out to the lake, to the bench, left of the middle. As they sat down, Dink pulled out his fingernail clippers and started trimming his nails. Edward just stared at him in disbelief. Dink noticed the stare and said, "I'll let you cut my toenails if you want to."

"No! I don't want to, and I can hardly believe you're doing that in front of me."

"Well, what's wrong with it? Dink said, "There's nothing dirty about fingernails!" Edward's mouth was open, but no words came out. So Dink continued, "Fingernail problems cause 10% of skin problems, Ed. You've got to take care of them. Did you know that your middle fingernail grows faster than the others?" Dink clipped his middle fingernail as he said this, and the clipping snapped over and landed on Edward's shoe. He quickly kicked it off.

"And your fingernails grow faster than your toenails . . . but you probably already knew that. Right?"

Edward nodded 'yes' but said, "No."

"And your fingernails grow faster in summer than in winter. Do you know why, Ed?" Edward didn't answer, so Dink volunteered, "Because they get more vitamin E from the sun. You need to pay attention, Ed. Discolored nails reflect the health of your body. I bet you didn't know that if you took a nail clipping and placed it in a glass of Pepsi for four days, that it would totally dissolve."

Edward asked, "Why in the world would anyone know that? How do you know that? Have you tested it?" Edward smiled at his question until Dink answered,

"Yes."

Edward started to ask, "Really?" But he knew better. Then Dink continued,

"And you've seen pictures of these crazy women who have these insane, garish, long fingernails? Well, there was a guy in India one time that had fingernails 48 inches long! Think about that, Ed."

Edward didn't want to think about that, but he couldn't stop himself.

"And . . ." But Edward interrupted him and said,

"Enough about fingernails, just go ahead and finish yours. But please, don't cut your toenails in front of me."

"Ed, I'm crippled and paralyzed on one side. You know I can't cut my own toenails. In fact, I can only cut the fingernails on one of my hands. The manicurist does the others for me, costs $20! You could do it for free, Ed."

"Forget it, Dink." Dink started to say something else, but Edward repeated, "Forget it!"

When Dink finished trimming the nails on his right, paralyzed hand, he asked Edward if he wanted to stay and have dinner with him in the cafeteria. "My treat," Dink added.

"Thanks, Dink, that would be nice. Beats another night at McDonald's."

When they placed their food orders in the cafeteria, Dink asked, "Do you often eat at McDonald's, Ed?"

"Probably more than I should. I know that food probably isn't good for me . . . but it's just easy."

Dink said, "Just be careful what you get there. A McDonald's Caesar salad is more fattening than their hamburger. In fact, if you look at the McDonald's website for its workers, it tells them to avoid fast food."

Edward asked, "Are you sure about that?"

Dink was insulted. "Of course I'm sure! And I'll tell you what else . . . you'd have to walk for seven straight hours to burn off a Big Mac, Coke, and fries. Think about that the next time you go there, Ed. Or maybe you should start riding a horse! They won't serve you in the drive-thru if you're on horseback. Did you know that they used to sell pizzas back in the '70's, Ed?"

Edward perked up, "Yeah, I remember that. I didn't really like their pizzas."

"They make $75 million a day, Ed. Every day! That's how they can afford to open a new restaurant every 14.5 hours. Heck, they did a survey once which showed that more people recognize the golden arches than recognize the cross! Did you know that Bill Gates has a McDonald's Gold Card, for unlimited fast food? Bill Gates, for crying out loud."

Edward sighed and added, "Well, they are the largest restaurant chain in the world, Dink."

"No, they're not . . . Subway is. Get your facts straight, Ed. You know, when they opened the first drive-thru in Kuwait, the queue was 7 miles long. What's the world coming to? The Queen of England even owns a McDonald's near Buckingham Palace, Ed. The freaking Queen of England!

I'll tell you how crazy people are, Ed. There is a guy in the Guinness Book of World Records who set a record for eating his 28,788th Big Mac. How sick is that?"

Edward looked amazed, and asked, "How can you remember that?"

"Trust me, Ed. I wish I could forget it."

Edward enjoyed the vegetable plate he ordered. Dink ignored his bowl of soup. Edward wasn't sure if Dink's stomach was bothering him again, or the thoughts of McDonald's hamburgers had simply destroyed his appetite.

9

EDWARD DID, IN FACT, JOIN AN ONLINE DATING SERVICE. He filled out all the forms and only lied occasionally. He was very unspecific in any of the traits and attributes he was looking for in a woman. Except, to be honest, he really didn't want a big, fat one—but he left that option open. He wanted to be politically correct and not hurt anyone's feelings. The only question he was adamant about was that he didn't want to date a woman who smoked. Other than that, he was wide open to the possibilities of meeting someone. He didn't even care how old they were.

That afternoon, he told Dink what he'd done to get his reaction, and Dink thought for a moment, then said, "You made a wise choice, Ed. Smoking causes 1 in every 5 deaths in the U.S. every year. A single cigarette contains 69 chemicals which are known to cause cancer. And people know that, Ed. Yet, every day, nearly 4,000 teens will smoke their first cigarette. While 1,000 of them get hooked on a daily habit.

And what totally amazes me, Ed is that some of the poorest people out there are the heaviest smokers. The average smoker in the U.S. spends between $1,500 and $3,300 a year on cigarettes, Ed. They can't buy food or clothes, but they sure buy smokes!" Edward started to say something, but Dink continued before he could gather his thoughts.

"And it's not just them they're hurting, Ed. Second-hand smoke causes nearly 50,000 deaths each year in our country. Ed, listen to this: 15 billion cigarettes are smoked worldwide, every day! And more than a third of all the world's smokers are Chinese. It's hard to understand . . . even Freud couldn't stop the habit. He never quit smoking cigars despite having over thirty cancer surgeries because of it . . . he just couldn't stop. You don't smoke do you, Ed?"

"No, sir, I don't. Never even tried it."

"Good for you. Smoking makes the risk of having a heart attack 200%-400% greater than that of non-smokers, Ed. If you're going to smoke anything, smoke marijuana! It's less harmful than tobacco or alcohol."

Edward thought about responding to that but thought better of it. Then Dink asked him, "You never even tried smoking? Not even once?"

"No, sir. I was afraid my parents would smell it on my clothes and punish me."

Dink scrunched up his face a little, then asked, "What about when you were an adult? You never tried it then . . . not even once when you were a little tipsy?"

Edward answered, "I've never been a little tipsy. I never drank much, Dink."

Dink's frown deepened as he tried to digest that information. They both stared out at the lake, and even though there were no birds there at the moment . . . they still stared at it. Then Dink added, "Online dating is good, Ed, one-third of all married couples met online." Then, and only then, did Edward smile.

That sat in silence, the kind of silence that was not awkward; rather the kind of silence that was comforting between two friends. After several minutes, they noticed Johnny, the attendant, wheeling another resident, in a wheelchair, towards one of the open benches near them. They watched him settle the wheelchair and secure it, then ask the older lady if she needed anything else. Then he passed near them humming a tune they could both hear. Upon hearing Johnny hum, Edward and Dink both looked at each other and Edward blurted out, "Louie, Louie . . . you probably don't know that one, Dink."

Dink's entire body jerked to attention as he blurted out, "Don't know it? Is that what you said? Because I'm old, you don't think I know stuff? Let me ask you something . . . do you know who sang that song, Edward?"

Edward didn't know who sang that song, but he couldn't answer because he was still in shock that Dink had called him 'Edward' rather than 'Ed.'

Dink waited about three seconds for an answer, then said, "The Kingsmen!" Then he sat back and continued, "That song was infamous because it was investigated by the FBI for supposedly 'dirty lyrics.'" He knew he had Edward's attention now, so he resumed, "Back in 1964 the FBI was alerted to pornographic lyrics on the airwaves. No one really knew who started the rumor, but it got to the point where they had to take a look at it. Some parents of teenagers wrote that the lyrics were 'filthy' and should be banned and the song's writer should be arrested.

The FBI played the song at 78 rpm, 45 rpm, and 33 1/3 rpm and even slower speeds, and their conclusions were that at every speed, the lyrics were totally unintelligible. In reality, the song revolved around a sailor from the Caribbean lamenting to a bartender named Louie about missing his far-away love. However, when the Kingsmen recorded it under crummy conditions, the lyrics which read, 'A fine little girl, she wait for me . . . ' came out sounding like 'A phlg mlmrl hlurl, duh vvvr me.'

Maybe because of all the uproar, or maybe just because it was a catchy tune, at any rate, the song would go on to become one the most covered songs in rock-and-roll history." When he finished, Dink looked back over at Ed who was speechless. Edward didn't know what to say, but he was thinking,

"How does this old, crippled, half-paralyzed man know about 'Louie, Louie?"

Apparently, Dink could read Edward's mind. He said, "Ed, music is an important part of history. Back when 'Louie, Louie' came out, another important aspect of the music industry was just beginning—Motown. The man behind Motown Records was a man named Berry Gordy . . . remember that name, Ed. He had a small record company that was going nowhere, then he signed a young girl named Mary Wells and together, they made history."

Edward asked, "Who?"

"Mary Wells, Ed. Pay attention. She sang Motown's first #1 hit back in 1964, 'My Guy.'"

Edward perked up and said, "Yeah, I know that song . . ." then he started trying to sing it, but had forgotten most of the words.

"They had a few other songs together back then, and in 1964 Mary Wells was the most important woman at Motown. She even had the Supremes and the Temptations singing backup on her songs—that's how important she was. But, she left Motown and digressed back to mediocrity. Motown, however, went on to release another 32 #1 hits in the next ten years. Poor Mary Wells never found that magic she had with 'My Guy,' and she eventually died of throat cancer at the age of only 49 . . . how sad."

Edward also thought that was sad, in a karma sort of way . . . but he was more interested in remembering the words to "My Guy." He kept singing to himself, "Do do do do, do do do do . . . My Guy." As Dink was reflecting on life and history and music, while silently staring out into the lake, Edward quickly googled the lyrics to "My Guy" on his iPhone. When he pulled it up, he sat there reading them, singing to himself, imagining that a woman he just met from the online dating service, was singing them to him:

"Nothing you can say,
Can tear me away,
From my guy.
Nothing you could do,
'cause I'm stuck like glue,
   To my guy.
I'm sticking to my guy,
Like a stamp to a letter,
Like birds of a feather,
We, stick together,
I'm tellin you from the start,
I can't be torn apart from my guy . . ."
A guy can dream.

10

THE FOLLOWING DAY, AS EDWARD PARKED HIS CAR, he saw Dink sitting out near the lake on the bench, left of the middle, with another older gentleman. He wondered if he should disturb them as he watched them for a few moments. Then he noticed something . . . neither man had moved—not a muscle. He walked towards them and came up on the side of the other gentleman and noticed he was sitting there fast asleep. He wasn't dead because Edward could tell he was breathing. Dink was staring out at the lake. When he noticed Edward standing there, he said, "Sit down, don't mind him, he's oblivious to everything."

So Edward sat between the two older men—one of them unconscious, the other one apparently lost in thought. Dink continued his gaze into the lake without saying anything else. At least there were a few ducks out there today, but it seemed as though they may be asleep as well. Edward sat there at least fifteen minutes without Dink saying anything. The other man would twitch occasionally. Finally, Edward asked, "Is everything okay?"

"Yeah. Just thinking."

Edward nodded and replied, "Thinking about what?"

"Elvis."

Edward hesitated a few seconds, then asked, "Elvis Presley?"

"Do you know any other Elvis's, Ed?"

"Why are you thinking about Elvis?

"I met him once, in Vegas when he was performing there. I was always a little sad about what happened to him."

Edward leaned forward and looked directly at Dink and asked, "You met Elvis in Vegas?"

"Yes. Am I not speaking clearly, Ed?"

"How did you happen to meet him?"

"Ed, did you know that Elvis didn't write any of his songs. He recorded over six hundred songs, but he didn't write any of them."

"But, how did you meet him?"

"And he recorded fifteen songs with the word 'Blue' in the title. That's a little strange, don't you think?"

"Yeah, I guess it is. But how did you meet him, Dink?"

"He's been dead a long time now, Ed, but he's still considered the best-selling artist of all time, with over 500 million records sold. He has 106 Gold albums, more than any other singer. Yet still, in 1954, two years before his big break, he auditioned for an amateur gospel quartet and was turned down."

Edward was still leaning forward, staring at Dink, but Dink ignored him and continued, "Did you know that his hair was naturally brown, Ed? He dyed it dark black because he thought he looked better that way. He also made thirty-three movies in his career—people forget about that. But you know something odd about him, Ed? He never performed outside of North America. Isn't that strange?"

At that point, the other older gentleman sighed and opened his eyes. He looked at Edward and asked, "Who are you?"

Dinked chimed in and said, "He's with me! Go back to sleep, Earl." And Earl did.

Dink continued, "There's only one home in the entire country that gets more visitors than Graceland, Ed. The White House. And did you know that nearly thirty years after his death, that he still had a number one song? That's amazing!"

Edward still wanted to know how Dink met Elvis, but he wanted to make sure Dink was finished . . . he wasn't.

"He affected a lot of people, Ed; and not just regular folks either. A lot of celebrities tried to copy him, but there was only one Elvis. Johnny Cash used to impersonate him all the time. And Bruce Springsteen, do you know who that is, Ed?"

"Yes."

"Well, before he got to be famous, he jumped over the fence at Graceland, trying to meet Elvis, but was caught by security guards. And one time Jerry Lee Lewis, I know you don't know him, he tried to break through the gates in a drunken rage, waving a pistol at everybody. No, Ed, there was nobody like Elvis."

At this point, Dink took a long breath and closed his eyes. Edward still wanted to know how he came to meet Elvis, but he decided to let his friend relive the memories of the King a little longer. The older gentleman started snoring and Dink's eyes were closed, and after a few minutes, Edward was wondering if he should leave them to their thoughts. Just then, the other gentleman sneezed, and everyone became wide awake again. Earl, the older gentleman, rose and said, "I'm going in."

Edward rose and said, "Nice to meet you, sir." Dink ignored him, and Earl ambled away. When Edward sat back down, he asked again, "Dink, exactly how did you meet Elvis?"

Dink never looked over at Edward, he kept staring out at the ducks on the lake, and answered, "I met Cher, too. I bet you didn't know that she never graduated high school, did you? Or, that she's worth over $300 million. Not bad for a girl who used to be a backup singer for groups like The Ronettes and the Righteous Brothers, is it, Ed? You know who Cher is, don't you?"

"Yes, Dink. I know who Cher is?"

"She married that crazy Sonny Bono, who was eleven years older than her, but she never loved him . . . I know she didn't. Did you know that he was mayor of Palm Springs and a U.S. Congressman before he died?"

"No. I did not know that, Dink."

"Yeah, old Cher did alright for herself. In fact, she's the only female artist in history to have had number one singles in the 1960's, 70's, 80's, and 90's. And she was pretty, too. Didn't you think so, Ed?"

Edward leaned back against the bench and said, "Yeah, Dink. She was pretty."

After a few quiet minutes, Dink started to get up from the bench and said, "Let's go inside have some cheese and wine."

Edward rose, but said, "I won't be able to Dink. I've got a date with one of the women I met from the online dating service." What he didn't tell Dink was that he was so nervous he couldn't feel his toes, nor had he slept in two nights. The thought of going on a date, after eleven years, was daunting, frightening, and downright intimidating. He'd thought all day of canceling this so-called date; which was really only meeting for coffee at TJ's Deli.

She seemed like a nice woman. A couple of years older than him, not pretty—but not ugly either. Plain-looking, like he was. He couldn't tell too much from her online picture, but her face seemed a little plump, and her smile seemed a little sad.

When Dink heard this news, he sat back down and demanded, "Tell me about her!" So, Edward sat back down and told Dink all he knew about Sylvia—that was her name. When he finished telling all he knew, Dink asked, "Does she smoke?"

Edward looked over at him and with a solemn voice replied, "Well, if she does, I'll slow down and use a lubricant."

Dink immediately picked up his walking cane and rapped Edward across the shin with it, saying, "Don't get smart with me young man."

"Ouch! That hurt."

"Good! Now answer the question: Does she . . . is she a . . . does she use tobacco products?"

"Her profile says 'no.'"

"How's her portfolio?"

"Now, Dink . . . how in the world would I know something like that?"

"Well, you have to look out for gold-diggers, Ed. Does she have big boobs?"

"I've got to go. I'll see you tomorrow."

Ed rose, but Dink stayed seated, then looked up at him and said, "If you need any help tonight, just give me a call. You can tell her about Elvis if you want to . . . Cher too."

"Thanks, Dink. That might come in handy."

11

EDWARD AND SYLVIA MET ON THEIR DATE at TJ's Deli and had a fine time. Not a great time. Not a bad time. It was just fine. Probably not as bad as either had anticipated, but also, not as good as they dreamed it might be. And, the more they talked to each other, the better it became. Sylvia was a little plumper than her picture showed, but Edward was probably not as idealistic as his five-year-old picture showed either.

In the course of the date, Edward told her about Dink and all the conversations he'd been having. Whether she was just being polite, or actually wanted to meet Dink, was unsure. But Edward told her he'd take her over to meet him as soon as it could be arranged. Their second "date" would be a lunch on Saturday and then a meeting at Arbor Acres with Dink. They shook hands when they left TJ's Deli and Edward thought to himself: "Hmm, not bad. I think she likes me."

Sylvia thought: "Well, nothing at all like his picture. Not sure I like him or not. And, why does he want me to meet this old man?"

When Edward saw Dink the next day, the first thing Dink asked was, "How did it go?"

Edward smiled and replied, "How did what go?"

Dink didn't respond, he just scowled at Edward until Edward answered. "It was fine. She's a little heavier than I thought, but she has a pretty face and we had a lot in common."

"Like what?"

Edward arched his eyebrows and said, "Huh?"

"You said you had a lot in common. What?"

43

Edward stuttered a little, then coughed, and finally replied, "Umm, we both like good movies. And we like to go out to eat—at good places! And . . . we'd both like to get a new SUV one day."

Dink completely shifted in his seat and turned to face Edward, then said, "You've just described 90% of the population in America. Isn't there anything unique about her? Was her hair pretty? Did she dress sexy? Does she have nice legs? Is she funny? Is she smart? Give me something to work with, Ed."

Edward perked up and said, "Yeah, she wants to meet you, Dink. I'm bringing her over here Saturday. That's okay, isn't it?"

Dink quickly stood up and walked right in front of Edward and replied, "You met a woman and you want to bring her over to visit an old, crippled, man with a bad personality? What's wrong with you, son?"

Dink didn't wait for an answer, he started shuffling off towards the wine and cheese area. Edward watched him stop twice and look for pennies, then open the door and look back and yell out, "Are you coming or not?"

Edward caught up with him as Dink was settling in with a plate of cheese squares and a glass of red wine. Edward sat down empty-handed because he was totally unsure where he stood in Dink's evaluation of him right now. Dink took a sip of wine and asked, "Do you know why they called Alexander the Great, great?"

"No, sir."

"Because, Ed, in fifteen years of conquests, he never lost a battle. And, he was smart. Most people don't know that he was tutored by Aristotle himself. Ed, he was simultaneously the King of Macedonia, Pharaoh of Egypt, King of Persia, and King of Asia! He founded seventy cities and had a least twenty named after himself, and one after his horse. And he did all this in only twelve years, Ed. Twelve years! He died when he was only 32 years old."

Dink was silent for a few moments, then continued, "He once held a drinking contest among his soldiers. When it was over, forty-two people had died from alcohol poisoning. Fidel Castro named three of his sons after Alexander the Great: Alexis, Alejandro, and Alexander. And speaking of Castro . . . when he took over Cuba, did you know that he immediately ordered all games sets of Monopoly to be destroyed?"

Dink stared over at Edward until Edward finally answered, "No, I didn't know that, Dink."

"And, did you know that Christopher Columbus once punished a man found guilty of stealing corn by having his ears and nose cut off and then selling the man into slavery? People think Columbus was so great, well let me tell you, Ed, over three million people perished from war, slavery, and the mines in Hispaniola under the rule of Christopher Columbus."

"Dink . . . why are you telling me all this odd stuff?"

Dink looked over at Edward and answered that question, "Exactly! And you want to bring a woman over to meet ME?" Dink then popped a cheese square into his mouth, but he threw it in so hard that he got choked. Edward quickly got up and slapped him on the back until Dink regained his breath and composure.

Later that night, Edward was sitting on his couch at home thinking about that question. Sure, Dink was a little strange. Of course, he was difficult. Yes, he could be a jerk sometimes. But, still, he wouldn't have to carry the conversation with Sylvia. Dink would tell her stories and all sorts of weird facts. It would take a lot of pressure off a second date, and he could silently evaluate Sylvia and see how she handled things and if she truly did like him or not. Yep . . . Sylvia had to meet Dink. It would be fine.

Each day, leading up to Saturday's meeting with Dink and Sylvia, became more and more bizarre.

Monday: "Ed, did you know that at any given time, 0.7% of the world is drunk. So, 50 million people are drunk right now. One time a Scotsman drank sixty pints of beer and had a hangover that lasted four weeks. And speaking of Scotland, there is more Guinness beer drunk in Nigeria than in Ireland.

Ed, they serve beer at McDonald's in France, Germany, Austria, Spain, and the Netherlands—did you know that?"

"No, Dink. I've never been over there."

Tuesday: "Ed, do you know who Babe Ruth is?"

"Yeah, Dink, I know who Babe Ruth is."

"Really? Did you know that he won seven World Series titles? That he had 714 home runs? That he won the home run title twelve times? And that he had two 20-win seasons as a pitcher, Ed? But listen to this: in 1920, he hit 54 home runs; the second place guy hit 19. In 1921, he hit 59 home runs, with the next nearest guy hitting only 24. And in some years he hit more home runs than entire teams did! Did you know all that, Ed?"

"No, sir."

Wednesday: "In Japan, there is a psychological disorder called the 'Paris Syndrome.' It's suffered by Japanese people, caused after realizing Paris isn't what they expected it to be. It's no better here, Ed . . . 35% of American workers said they would forgo a pay raise in exchange for having their boss fired! Ed, you know what's really sad? Wal-Mart has a lower acceptance rate than Harvard University . . . it's true. And, Ed, I don't want to scare you with this, but I thought you might want to know . . . in 2007, a couple from Bosnia, divorced after discovering they both had an online affair with each other under fake names."

Thursday: "Ed, 1/3 of the earth's surface is partially or totally desert. And Antarctica is the largest desert in the world. Even bigger than the Sahara Desert, which is so big that it would stretch farther than the distance from New York to Los Angeles. Ed, there was a famous tree, called the Tree of Tenere, that was considered the most isolated tree on earth. It was the only tree for 250 miles in the Sahara Desert. A drunk driver hit that tree in 1973 and knocked it down."

Edward couldn't take anymore. He took Friday off and was beginning to think that the meeting between Dink and Sylvia might not be the best idea he'd ever had.

12

LUNCH ON SATURDAY FOR EDWARD AND SYLVIA was a bit awkward, with long stretches of silence between them. If it hadn't been for the waitress asking if they wanted more sweet tea, it would have been unbearable. Edward was harboring great anxiety and trepidation about the upcoming meeting with Dink. Sylvia was wondering if this meeting was some sort of audition for the privilege of dating Edward. They were both too nervous for dessert.

Edward parked the car and saw Dink sitting out by the lake, left of the middle, on his usual bench. They walked up and Edward made the introductions and they all sat down to stare at the lake, which had two geese swimming around the near edge. Sylvia said, "I've heard so much about you, Mr. Cleveland, I feel like I know you already."

Dink replied, "I'm not sure if that's a compliment or not, but thank you, young lady. And you can call me Dink like Ed does."

Sylvia smiled and answered, "I'd prefer, Mr. Cleveland, if you don't mind. My parents always taught me to respect my elders."

"I appreciate that Sylvia and I'm impressed with your parents already; but still, I prefer Dink."

Sylvia smiled and said, "I wanted to ask you a question, Mr. Cleveland, I was wondering if you knew that during WW1, a British soldier spared the life of a wounded German. That German's name was Adolph Hitler."

Dink shifted a bit in his seat and looked directly at Sylvia as she continued, "And that Hitler suffered from chronic flatulence and took 28 different drugs to fight it. Plus, he only had one testicle. Before WWII, he was nominated for the Nobel Peace Prize in 1939, and in 1938 he was Time Magazine's 'Man of the Year.'"

Still no response from Dink. Edward was sweating bullets. Sylvia resumed, "He also suffered from ailurophobia, which is the fear of cats, the same phobia that one of your heroes suffered from-- Alexander the Great. The American secret service tried to spike Hitler's food with female hormones to feminize him . . . it never worked."

Edward broke in her dialogue and said, "That's all great stuff, Sylvia, but . . ."

Sylvia paid no attention to Edward and continued, "Before the Holocaust, Hitler gave the U.S., Great Britain, and many other nations a chance to take in Jewish refugees. They all refused. And when the D-Day forces landed in France, Hitler was asleep. None of his generals dared send re-enforcements without his permission, and no one dared wake him. The place where he ultimately killed himself in Berlin is now a children's playground."

She paused for a moment and Dink asked, "Anything else?"

"Yes, Mr. Cleveland, Hitler was obsessed with the American Old West. And twice before the war, Churchill went to Munich to meet Hitler at a hotel. Hitler stood him up both times and the most famous two men of the war never met."

Dink nodded and rubbed his chin, then said, "It's Dink. And Ed, why don't you know history as well as this young lady does?"

Edward responded, "Sounds like she knows more than you, Dink."

Dink smiled a crooked little mischievous smile, and said, "But does she also know that when Hitler was in prison, he wrote to a Mercedes dealership begging for a car loan? And, that when he was young and lived in Vienna, that he and Stalin, Trotsky, Tito, and Freud all lived within a few miles of each other, and often visited the same coffeehouses?"

Edward was speechless . . . he didn't know whether to try and answer for Sylvia, keep his mouth shut, or jump in the lake. They both looked at Sylvia, who answered, "Yes, Mr. Cleveland, I knew that."

There was a truce. They all leaned back, took a breath, and stared at the two geese in the lake. After several silent minutes, Dink said, "It's obvious you've read quite a bit, Sylvia. Did you know that people who read books live an average of almost two years longer than those who don't read at all? And speaking of long life . . . another study showed that working past age sixty-five leads to a longer life. And that a half hour of physical activity, six days a week, is linked to 40% lower risk of early death. And a lack of exercise is now causing as many deaths as smoking across the world."

Sylvia never took her eyes off the geese, but answered, "Yes, Mr. Cleveland . . . I knew that."

Edward figured now would be the opportune time to butt in, "Well, this has been great. I guess we'd better be leaving, Sylvia. Thanks for inviting us over, Dink."

Dink frowned and replied, "I didn't invite you over. But I'm glad she came. You could learn something from her, Ed."

Sylvia smiled and answered, "Okay, Edward. Nice meeting you, Mr. Cleveland."

Dink said, "Dink!"

She smiled and starting walking away with Edward when Dink called out, "Ed, just a minute, something I need to tell you."

Edward stopped and walked back to Dink, who told him, "You'd better keep her . . . but tell her my name is Dink! You got it?"

Edward nodded and turned to catch up with Sylvia, who was checking her iPhone while she waited. When they were in the car, driving out of the complex, Edward said, "Well that was interesting. What did you think?"

"I've had a lovely day, Edward. Why does he call you Ed?"

The following afternoon, Edward stopped in to see Dink in his apartment. Before saying "Hello" or "How are you?" The first thing Dink asked was, "Did you kiss her?"

"That's really none of your business, Dink."

"You didn't, did you? Ed, what am I going to do with you?"

They were both looking out Dink's large bay window at the lake where several ducks had just landed. Dink said, "Anatidaephobia is the weird fear that somewhere, somehow, a duck is watching you."

"Dink . . . I don't believe that. I'm sorry, I just don't believe it!"

Dink shuffled over to his computer, Googled "anatidaephobia" and called Edward over to look at the screen. Sure enough, Google confirmed, it's the weird fear that somewhere, somehow, a duck is watching you. Edward read it, then looked out the window and was almost certain he saw one of the ducks in the lake staring at him.

13

THE FOLLOWING WEDNESDAY, Sylvia invited Edward to her house for a homemade dinner. Edward was thrilled at the prospect of a delicious meal and the thoughts of maybe even a goodnight kiss . . . a man could dream. When he arrived at 1320 N. Columbus, he found it to be a tidy, little house in a quaint neighborhood in the West End section of Winston-Salem. He liked it and could picture himself living in a neighborhood like this—even a house like this.

Sylvia invited him into the small living room and guided him to the couch, where she had two glasses of sweet tea sitting on coasters on the small table in front of them. As soon as they sat down, Sylvia said, "Edward, are you familiar with Albert Einstein?"

Edward thought that was an odd question, but he answered, "I know who he is if that's what you mean."

She began, "He didn't even speak until he was three years old. Today, there is a term for that called the 'Einstein Syndrome,' which is used to describe exceptionally bright people whose speech is delayed. But back then, they thought he was just 'slow.' His teachers didn't consider him a good student at all. One of the reasons for that was because he had a very poor memory and had a terrible time just remembering simple things like names, dates, and phone numbers.

But he always said, 'Imagination is more important than knowledge, for knowledge is limited, but imagination encircles the world.' As he grew up, he needed at least ten hours of sleep to function well. And, he was an avid smoker; he even credited smoking his pipe with calming him and giving him better judgment."

Edward sat there wondering what in the world was happening. He took a small sip of his tea, thought it was too sweet, and quickly sat it down as Sylvia continued, "He never drove a car in his life. Don't you think that's a bit odd? But the women seemed to love him, he was never at a loss for female companionship. But he was strange, Edward. Before he married his first wife, he made a list of conditions which she had to agree to and sign off on. This marriage lasted sixteen years, which is a miracle when you look at the list of conditions he made his wife adhere to:

All my clothes and laundry are kept in good order

I will receive three meals regularly in my room

My bedroom and study will be kept neat, and especially that my desk is left for my use only

And, you will renounce all personal relations with me insofar as they are not completely necessary for social reasons.

He also made her sign a contract that said she would leave the room or stop talking to him if he told her to.

And she agreed to all of them. Can you believe that, Edward?"

Before Edward could actually answer, she continued, "But somehow women kept being drawn to him. Even after his second marriage, which was to his first cousin, by the way, he maintained connections with six women, receiving gifts and spending time with them. Amazing!

He could've lived longer than he did. Before he died, doctors suggested surgery, since he suffered from a burst blood vessel. However, he refused, stating, 'It is tasteless to prolong life artificially.' When he died, they kept his brain in a jar for many years. And they also kept his eyes, which are now located in a safety deposit box in New York City."

Sylvia stopped momentarily and took a drink of sweet tea, then finished up her discourse on Einstein by telling Edward, "He was offered the Presidency of Israel, which he politely turned down. And when he published his 'Theory of Relativity,' the New York Times sent their golfing correspondent to interview him. Einstein was so smart that he was able to make this golfer understand exactly what he was talking about."

Then, Sylvia picked her glass of sweet tea, stood up, and said, "I hope you're hungry. We're having fried fish."

In between less than succulent bites of fried fish, Edward learned, from Sylvia, that:

The only member of the band "ZZ Top" without a beard, is Frank Beard.

The inventor of Vaseline used to eat a spoonful of it every day.

A snail can sleep for three years.

Half of all airline pilots surveyed admitted to having fallen asleep while flying a passenger plane.

You burn more calories sleeping than you do watching television.

The average person falls asleep in seven minutes.

A study found that people who frequently take naps tend to die younger than those who don't.

Cats sleep for 70% of their lives, whereas, giraffes only need 5-30 minutes of sleep a day.

Junk mail in the U.S. destroys 100 million trees per year.

But, scientists discovered that there are 8 times more trees on earth than we previously thought.

And, finally . . . thank, God for that, 1 in 8 young people in Britain have never seen a live cow!

Edward was so overwhelmed with trivia and useless information that he completely abandoned the thought of a goodnight kiss. He settled on a firm, yet friendly, handshake from Sylvia. As he started walking towards his car, she called out to him, "Oh, Edward . . . when do you think we can visit Mr. Cleveland again?"

Edward half-stopped and replied, "I'll check on it and let you know. Thanks again for the fish, Sylvia. Goodnight."

As soon as Edward arrived in the safe, quiet confines of his home, he sat in front of the computer and scrolled through the online dating website. Surely, there had to be a woman out there who was not the female clone of Dink. He found several possibilities, while also feeling a bit guilty concerning Sylvia. He didn't really want to "not" see Sylvia any longer . . . he just wanted another option, maybe. Sylvia was nice. She had a pretty face. She was smart . . . he kept looking a little longer.

Of course, at his next meeting with Dink, he wanted to know all about the dinner date with Sylvia. "Did you hold hands?"

"No."

"Did you make out?"

"No, Dink, we didn't make out . . . geez!"

Dink sighed and said, "Well, there's no use in me asking my next question then. I need to have a long talk with you, Ed, regarding women."

Edward rolled his eyes but remained silent. Dink, thinking he needed to lighten the conversation, changed the subject and said, "Have you ever heard of Bob Marley?" He waited for an answer, but Edward was silent, so he continued, "On what was to be his next-to-last concert, which happened to be in New York City at Madison Square Garden, he shared the bill that evening with the Commodores—strange pairing. For him, the concert was a great success and he greatly overshadowed the costume wearing, choreographed dancing Commodores.

Only days after his triumphant American concert, he was out jogging in Central Park, and he collapsed and had to be taken to the hospital. It was a grim diagnosis: a cancerous growth from an old soccer injury on his big toe had metastasized and spread to his brain, liver, and lungs. Less than eight months later, at age thirty-six, he died. He never really knew the fame that would follow throughout the years. It was a sad, tragic thing, Ed."

Edward finally spoke, "Why do you know about Bob Marley? I thought you'd only be interested in someone like Beethoven."

"Ed, a man needs to be well-rounded. I do know about Beethoven. His father recognized his genius but was hard on the young boy. He forced him to practice day and night and stood over him as Beethoven played and cried. His life was never easy. Some women thought him a genius, while others found him repulsive. One woman called him 'ugly and half crazy.' Throughout his life he was sickly. He suffered from deafness, colitis, rheumatism, typhus, skin disorders, abscesses, jaundice, hepatitis, and cirrhosis of the liver. And, he also began to hear constant buzzing at age 27 that never left him.

He never married and died a bachelor. He led a brilliant, yet tortured life, Ed. Somewhat similar to Tupac."

"What? Tupac? You mean the rapper?" Edward was flummoxed.

"Well, that wasn't his real name, he changed it to that. He went to a school of the arts and took ballet classes. I bet you never knew that, did you, Ed? He also auditioned for the role of 'Bubba' in the movie 'Forrest Gump,' but he didn't get it. Before he was killed, he briefly dated Madonna, but his 'posse' made him dump her when they started questioning why he was going out with a white girl.

The night he was shot, he struggled trying to get out of the car he was riding in. A police officer tried to obtain information from him to identify the shooter, but the officer said that Tupac looked at him and only said, 'F**k you.' He slipped into unconsciousness and died a few days later. They've never caught the guy who shot him, Ed. Pretty sad, don't you think?"

All Edward could think was, "How does this old, crippled, paralyzed man know about Tupac and Bob Marley?"

14

TWO DAYS LATER, Edward said, "Dink, I'm still surprised you knew about Tupac and Bob Marley. That's pretty amazing!"

"No, it's not, Ed. Men should broaden their horizons, not be confined only to what they're comfortable with. Do I like Tupac's music? Frankly, no. Some of Marley's stuff is okay, but I like a lot of the Stones stuff."

"The Rolling Stones? You like the Rolling Stones?"

"Yes, Ed. I wasn't always old, you know. I've sort of identified with Mick Jagger a little."

Edward's mouth dropped open as he said, "Really?"

"Yes, he's very smart. When they first started out in 1962, they were just a cover band, then the Beatles told them the only way to make serious money was to write their own songs. That's how Mick and Keith Richards started. Do you know who Keith Richards is, Ed?"

"Yeah, Dink, I know him."

"Well, they wrote 'As Tears Go By' and sold it to Marianne Faithful in 1964 and that started them on their way. You know, Jagger is rumored to have slept with over 4,000 women, but, it's probably more. He's admitted to sleeping with Angelina Jolie, Uma Thurman, Farrah Fawcett, and Carly Simon—you know, she wrote that song about him—'You're So Vain.' Heck, he and some thirty-year-old girl just had a baby when Mick was 73! It's rumored he's paying nearly $20,000 a month in child support.

I really only had one misgiving about the Stones. Do you remember Brian Jones, Ed?"

"Brian Jones? No . . . who is he?"

"He was one of the founding members of the Stones and was responsible for the innovative music of theirs all through the 60's. He could play anything. They said he could learn to play a completely new instrument in only one day. As they got to be world famous, the lifestyle ruined him. He couldn't stop drinking and drugging. He was barely functional in the end. Instead of trying to encourage their friend get help of some sort, Jagger and Richards went to his house one day in 1969 and fired him from the band. Less than a month later, he was found dead in the swimming pool in his backyard. They should've helped him, Ed . . . they should've helped him."

Edward nodded but, of course, he had no answer to that inconceivable question. After a few minutes, they walked outside to the lake and sat on the bench. Dink found a penny on the way. Nothing was floating on the water except some leaves. Edward finally commented, "I didn't know you were so interested in music, Dink. That's pretty cool."

Dink turned to look at him and said, "Cool? It's just being cognizant of your surroundings, Ed, and being interested in the world around you. Not being cool. Whatever that means. Music is important, Ed. You need to learn that. The type of music you listen to affects the way you perceive the world. Music triggers activity in the same brain structure that releases the 'pleasure chemical' dopamine during sex and eating. People who have had severe brain injuries can recall personal memories when listening to music. But it can be dangerous, Ed."

"What can be dangerous? Music?"

"Yes, Ed. The lifespan of a rock star is 25 years shorter than the average person. And, over 19% of rock musicians die from suicide. Whereas over 51% of hip-hop artists are murdered. Either way, they're both dead. Musicians have the same life expectancy as Zimbabweans: the lowest on earth.

I know you won't believe this, Ed, but last year Mozart sold more CD's than Beyoncé did."

Edward looked a bit shocked, so Dink added, "You don't need to look it up—it's true."

They both gazed into the lake a few moments, then Dink added, "Guess who the only father-daughter collaboration to hit #1 on the charts was?"

Edward thought about that, but he had no clue.

"Frank and Nancy Sinatra back in 1967, with 'Something Stupid.'" Dink actually smiled when he said that.

"Ed, did you know that white people consume nearly 80% of all rap music sold in the U.S.? Or, that Finland has more heavy metal bands per capita than any other country in the world? But guess what, Ed . . . for every $1,000 of music sold, the average musician makes just $23."

Edward kept staring into the lake, so Dink continued, "And here's one fact I have never understood, Ed, but it's true . . . Bob Marley, Jimi Hendrix, and Tupac never won a Grammy, but Milli Vanilli and Justin Bieber did. Now explain that one, Ed!"

Of course, Edward was completely dumbfounded by those facts. He thought to himself, "Justin Bieber??"

"Ed, it's been proven that babies remain calm twice as long when listening to a song as they do when listening to speech. And flowers can grow faster by listening to music. Music can be beneficial in other ways too, Ed. In 1989, the U.S. military blared AC/DC music at General Noriega's compound in Panama for two continuous days. The dictator surrendered without a fight. And, the British Navy uses Britney Spears' songs to scare off Somali pirates."

Edward was not surprised by all these facts known by Dink. But he was surprised when Dink asked, "You didn't like Sylvia very much, did you?"

Edward thought about that question for a bit too long, until Dink asked again, "Well?"

"It's not that I don't like her, Dink. But I'm not sure I REALLY like her either. Maybe there's someone else out there I'd like better."

Dink slowly nodded and replied, "Anyone in particular, or are you just doing some online shopping?"

"I'm not doing anything yet, but I might. And I might bring Sylvia back over here if you want me to."

Dink answered, "I'd like to talk with her again; she's smart. But I'm not the one who'll try to kiss her at the end of the evening either."

They both sat there thinking about those scenarios, until Dink finally spoke, "Ed, did you know that the majority of Canada's population lives south of Seattle?"

Edward seemed deep in thought and never responded, so Dink continued, "And when people have a kidney transplant, the old damaged kidney is left in the body. It would actually be more dangerous to remove it because they're located in a hard-to-reach area. They just place the new kidney in front of your pelvis and everything works fine."

Still no response from Edward, so he added, "It takes up to two years for a pineapple to grow to maturity, Ed." Still no movement from Edward. "Do you know the actor Matthew McConaughey, Ed?" Before Edward could answer, even if could've answered, Dink stated, "He has a brother who named his son Miller Lyte. The beer company gave him free Miller Lites for a year."

Edward finally stirred, "I think I will see Sylvia again . . . but also, I'll probably try to meet someone else."

Dink smiled and said, "Ed, you're the kind of man who could play a game of Russian Roulette with a fully loaded magnum, and win!"

15

As Edward was home, pondering his next move, watching "Jeopardy" on television, his phone rang. It was Sylvia asking him if he'd like to come over to her house and sit on the front porch. She'd just made some fresh lemonade and was thinking about him. The thought that a woman was actually thinking about him, got Edward a little excited. He told her he'd be right over.

It was a nice comfortable swing, with a blue, shaggy carpet in it for a cushion. They sat and she gave him a glass of sweet lemonade. It wasn't too sweet, like the tea was, but tasted just right. They started swinging and sipping in silence, then Sylvia gently put her hand next to Edward's hand, so that they were touching. Then she said, "Edward, I saw a show last night about Presidents. It was fascinating."

Edward took the bait and asked, "Which Presidents?" That was all it took.

"We often think the founding fathers were perfect men . . . but they had their ways, just like people do today. For instance, when John Adams was running for President against Thomas Jefferson, he called Jefferson a 'mean-spirited, low-lived fellow, the son of a half-breed Indian squaw, sired by a Virginia mulatto.'

And Grover Cleveland was a cradle-robber. He married the daughter of his law partner, at whose birth he was present. When his partner died, Cleveland became the girl's legal guardian. Several years later, they got married at the White House and had a child named Ruth. The namesake of the candy bar, Baby Ruth."

Sylvia took a moment to take another sip of lemonade, then moved her little finger on top of Edward's little finger, before continuing, "When Lewis and Clark were exploring the West, they had two young bear cubs sent back to President Jefferson. He kept them in a cage on the White House lawn and would take them for walks around town. But he wasn't as strange as Calvin Coolidge. Coolidge slept about ten hours a night and had a morning ritual where he enjoyed having Vaseline rubbed on his head while he ate breakfast in bed." She now moved her ring finger on top of Edward's ring finger and continued,

"John Quincy Adams used to skinny-dip in the Potomac River. And Warren Harding lost the White House China in a poker game. He loved to gamble, but he wasn't very good and on one hand, he bet all of the White House china—and lost! Whereas, Richard Nixon was the best poker player in his Navy unit. Within a few months, he had won around $6,000 in poker games, which he used to fund his first congressional campaign.

James A. Garfield was ambidextrous. He could write Greek with one hand, while at the same time, write Latin with the other." Her middle finger now covered Edward's middle finger as she said, "And even though about forty million emails were generated by Clinton staffers over the course of his presidency, President Clinton was more comfortable writing memos or making phone calls.

During his eight years in office, he reportedly sent only TWO emails. One was to the astronaut, John Glenn, who was aboard the Space Shuttle Discovery. The laptop Clinton used to send that email to Glenn was later auctioned for over $60,000." Sylvia now covered Edward's entire hand with her hand and finished her monologue with,

"In 1981, President Reagan was shot in Washington, D.C. He was hit by a single bullet that entered under his left underarm, stopping just shy of his heart. He nearly died. His lung had been punctured and internal injuries caused him to lose half of his blood.

Somehow, he maintained his sense of humor and told his wife, 'Honey, I forgot to duck.' Before the surgery, he was asked what he'd want on his gravestone if he didn't recover, he said, 'All in all, I'd rather be in Philadelphia.'

Years later, he was attending a birthday party at an air base in West Berlin when a balloon popped during the festivities. He snapped, 'Missed me!'"

When Edward was half-way certain she was finished, he called her name softly, and when she turned to face him, he kissed her. He hadn't planned it that way, it just happened that way. Sylvia blushed and Edward broke out in beads of sweat. Then Edward turned his hand over to hold Sylvia's hand tightly in his. She may have had more presidential stories to tell, but the thoughts of Edward's kiss had momentarily quieted her.

They sat and rocked in blissful silence . . . at least it was blissful to Edward. Then Sylvia asked, "Do you want more?"

Edward quickly replied, "No, that was enough presidential information for tonight. I like just sitting here with you."

Sylvia smiled and said, "That's not what I meant."

Edward and Sylvia retired inside to the sofa where they made out like two teenagers in heat. Edward's shirt was hopelessly wrinkled, and Sylvia's lipstick was all over Edward's face. For each of them—it was a long time coming. For each of them—it was a night they'd always remember. And, for each of them—they hoped there would be many more to follow.

The following day Edward was questioning himself concerning how much he should tell Dink about his evening with Sylvia. Dink was sitting on the bench, left of the middle when Edward walked up. Before he sat down, Dink started, "Ed, in 1972, a Yugoslav Airlines DC-9 departed from Copenhagen for Belgrade with twenty-eight passengers and crew. At an altitude of 33,000 feet, a bomb in the cargo section, planted by terrorists, exploded. The plane disintegrated and crashed in the mountains. A stewardess on the plane, named Vesna Vulovic survived the 33,000-foot fall by sitting on the tail of the plane.

The twenty-two-year-old Vulovic wasn't even supposed to be on that flight. It was a mix-up. However, she survived and ended up with a fractured skull, two broken legs, and three broken vertebrae—one of which was crushed and left her paralyzed from the waist down. Several operations later allowed her to walk and she became a celebrity, meeting

Paul McCartney and others. She's now a national hero in Serbia.

Luck was also on the side of a Serbian music teacher named Frane Selak. He survived a train wreck which killed 17 other passengers but escaped with only a broken arm and some bruises. A year later, he was flying when a door abruptly blew away from the cockpit and crashed the plane. 19 people were killed in that accident, but Selak landed in a haystack and had only minor injuries.

A few years later he was on a bus that plunged into an icy river. Four people died in that accident, but Selak emerged unharmed. A year later he was driving his car when the gas tank exploded and the car caught fire . . . again, he got out unharmed. Incredibly enough, the same thing happened to him three years later—car catches fire and explodes. This time he lost his hair in the fire—that's all.

In 1995, he was hit by a bus but left with only minor injuries. The following year he was driving on a mountain road and his car ran off the road over a 300-foot cliff. He jumped out of the door and landed in a tree, whereas the car crashed at the bottom. Then, after all that, in 2003, Selak won the million-dollar Croatian lottery, turning the man into either the world's unluckiest man or the world's luckiest one."

Dink then looked over at Edward and said, "Ed, my friend, you are not that lucky. You'd better thank your lucky stars Sylvia will even think about kissing you. Now let's go get a glass of wine."

Edward numbly sat there, not knowing what to think . . . how? Why? When?

Dink leaned down looking for what he thought was a penny, but it was just a piece of broken glass, then he yelled back, "Are you coming?"

When they sat down, before Dink started eating his cheese squares, Edward asked, "Why would you mention about Sylvia kissing me? That's very weird."

Dink was careful not to pop another cheese square in his mouth—no more choking. But he placed one in and slowly chewed it until he washed it down with a healthy sip of wine. Then he said, "No, Ed, that's not weird. Weird would be that when a male bee climaxes, his testicles explode and he dies. But a pig has an orgasm that lasts thirty minutes . . . that's weird. And think of this, Ed, 54 million people alive right now will be dead within twelve months!

And try and grasp this . . . a Nintendo had over twice the computing power of the first lunar lander. And, finally, Ed, this is weird: if you keep going North, you will eventually go South. But, if you keep going East, you will never go West.

It is not weird that I would know Sylvia and you would eventually kiss!"

16

THE FOLLOWING DAY WHEN EDWARD CALLED SYLVIA, he asked her if she had spoken with Dink. Of course, she hadn't, and she thought that was an odd question to be asking, given their previous night's history. They decided they would drop in and visit Dink before their dinner date that evening. Edward cautioned her, "Don't let him draw you into any trivia contests. That's what he likes to do."

"Edward, I'm quite capable of handling myself around Mr. Cleveland."

Edward shyly said, "Dink."

She, not so shyly, answered, "Mr. Cleveland."

When they arrived, Dink was sitting in the reception area reading a book and eating a cookie. They walked up to him and he closed the book, looked at Edward, then looked at Sylvia and said, "Japan has 50,000 people over one hundred years old. I'd be young if I lived there. Their birth rate is so low that adult diapers sell more than baby diapers. It also consists of over 6,800 islands . . . not many people know that."

Dink seemed proud of these facts until Sylvia added, "I know. I used to live there, my parents were missionaries. It was a bit odd over there—most streets in Japan have no names. And in Japan, tipping a server is considered rude."

Dink seemed flummoxed, temporarily, but then added, "Their criminal courts have a 99% conviction rate."

Sylvia added, "Well, it's a little easier over there, the likelihood of being killed by a gun is about the same as an American's chance of being killed by lightning. And they view things differently . . . the lone Japanese man who survived the Titanic was called a coward in his country for not dying with the others."

Dink smiled and replied, "They do see the world differently. The government had to build a fence around a volcano over there to stop a trend of over 2,000 people committing suicide by jumping in. And, in Japan, it's perfectly acceptable to sleep on the job. It's viewed as exhaustion from working so hard."

Sylvia nodded and added, "Edward, did you know that the number of Chinese killed by the Japanese during World War 11 is greater than the number of Jews killed in the Holocaust?"

Edward was smart enough not to get entangled in this dialogue. And he didn't have to, because Dink answered, "Over a quarter of all unmarried Japanese males, aged 30-40, are virgins."

"When I lived there we could buy eel flavored ice cream. And the beer cans had braille on them so blind people didn't confuse them with soft drinks."

Sylvia and Dink stared at each other, then Dink added in conclusion, "Over 100,000 Japanese disappear without a trace every year, many to save their honor after a divorce, job loss, failing an exam, or debt."

They continued their stare when Edward finally spoke up and said, "Why don't we get a glass of wine."

They all sat drinking a glass of red wine that was less than exhilarating. Edward wanted to put a couple of ice cubes in his, but he knew Dink would not approve. Dink wanted to put a couple of ice cubes in his, but he thought Sylvia would not approve. Sylvia thought the wine was delicious. Dink then asked Sylvia, "How long was your family in Japan?"

"Less than a year, Mr. Cleveland. Then we moved to Korea to a small town up north, near the border."

"Please call me Dink. Did you like Korea as well?"

"Our small church was a haven for refugees from North Korea, Mr. Cleveland. Most of the people I knew were from the north. In the last sixty years, over 23,000 North Koreans have defected to South Korea. Whereas only two South Koreans have gone to the North."

Dink started to say something, but Sylvia continued, "You know, marijuana is legal in North Korea and is not even classified as a drug. But wearing blue jeans is Illegal there."

Dink was silent, but Edward said, "I didn't know that. That's very interesting, Sylvia."

Dink stared a hole through Edward and Sylvia volunteered, "They hold elections every five years in North Korea, but the ballots only list one candidate. And up there, only military and government officials can own motor vehicles." Sylvia was looking directly at Dink, and said, "North Korea is the only nation in the world to currently have a U.S. Naval ship captured. Did you know that, Edward?"

Edward, of course, knew better than to answer that loaded question, so Sylvia continued, "When we were there, North Korea used a fax machine to send threats to South Korea. And back a few years ago, North Korea's President killed his own uncle by throwing him naked into a cage with 120 starving dogs. It's a poor country, Edward. Most of the people have next to nothing. In fact, Bill Gates' net worth is four and a half times as large as North Korea's estimated GDP."

Finally, Dink came alive, "Speaking of Bill Gates, he aimed to become a millionaire by the age of 30. However, he became a billionaire at 31. If he was a country, he would be the sixty-third richest country on earth. And yet, he has no college degree, even though his SAT score was 1590 out of 1600. He attended Harvard, but got bored and quit. But when he was there, he changed the school's program codes so that he was placed in classes with mostly female students . . . told you he was smart."

Dink was staring directly into Sylvia's eyes and said, "Ed, if Bill Gates spent a million dollars a day, it would take him 218 years to spend all his money. He was so smart, that at Microsoft, he used to memorize employee's license plates to keep tabs on their comings and goings. He recently told an interviewer that he's only leaving his kids $10 million each—just a fraction of his $81 billion net worth. He said, 'Leaving kids massive amounts of money is not a favor to them.' But, he has donated over $28 billion so far to charities."

Sylvia and Dink continued their stare down until Edward rose and said, "Who wants another glass of wine?"

They all had another glass of wine and the dialogue between Dink and Sylvia became a contest of wits, triviality, and absurdity. Edward sat dumbfounded and sipped his wine. Dink and Sylvia stared each other down as Dink started things, "Ed, half of the entire population of Australia lives in three cities: Sydney, Melbourne, and Brisbane."

Sylvia said, "Edward, did you know that there is enough fuel in a full tank of a jumbo jet to drive an average car four times around the world?" Before Edward could answer "No" to that question, Dink came up with,

"Beetles taste like apples, wasps like pine nuts, and worms taste like fried bacon. Do you like bacon, Ed?"

Sylvia: "Edward, did you know that a portion of the water you drink has already been drunk by someone else, probably several times over?"

Dink: "Ed, there are more stars in space than there are grains of sand on every beach in the world."

Sylvia: "For every human on earth, Edward, there are 1.6 million ants."

Dink: "Ed, think about this . . . John Tyler, the 10th President of the U.S. was born in 1790. He has a grandson that is alive today."

Sylvia, "Edward, guess what the percentage of wilderness is in Africa?" Before Edward could answer, she said, "28%. Now guess what the percentage of wilderness is in North America." Again, before he could answer, "38%."

When Sylvia answered that question for him, Edward, who had already finished his glass of wine, picked up Sylvia's glass and started drinking it as well.

Dink: "Dostoevsky wrote one of his greatest works to pay off a gambling debt. Did you know that, Ed?"

Edward just nodded his head and continued drinking.

Sylvia: "Well, Edward, did you know that while filming 'The Wizard of Oz,' 16-year old Judy Garland was put on a diet of chicken soup, coffee, and eighty cigarettes a day." It really wasn't a question, and she really didn't expect Edward to answer it, nor to say anything at all. And he didn't.

Dink: "Ed, when President Kennedy was killed, during the autopsy, his brain was removed and stored in the National Archive. His brain was subsequently lost and remains missing to this day."

At this point, Edward took one final last gulp of Sylvia's wine, finishing it, looked at them both and said, "Turtles can breathe out of their butts." And with that, Edward rose from his chair, took Sylvia's hand, pulled her up next to him, kissed her on the lips, and walked her out of the building.

17

THE NEXT MORNING EDWARD HAD A MASSIVE HEADACHE. He wasn't used to drinking wine like he did the night before. But, he went to work like the good boy he was, checking the wall clock repeatedly, wishing for 5:00. No Dink today. No Sylvia today. No . . . today was stop by Burger King, go home, take a shower, put my pajamas on and watch TV, day. And that's what he did.

He turned on the History Channel and found a special on Jack Nicholson. Why the History Channel was running a show on someone who wasn't dead yet confused Edward; but he liked Jack, so he watched it. He learned that Nicholson lived next door to Marlon Brando and Warren Beatty on Mulholland Drive on the block known as "Bad Boy Drive."

When Brando died, Nicholson bought his house, then razed it. He and Brando were good friends and Jack didn't want anyone else living there, so he paid over $5 million for the 3,040 square foot house. But he didn't keep it long. Instead, he reportedly demolished it and planted Brando's favorite flowers in its place. A tribute to his friend.

Nicholson once roamed around his own house for several months, completely nude. It was a form of "self-help therapy" he read about and wanted to try. Even when his own daughter visited, he stayed nude. He did interviews nude, entertained nude, and ate nude . . . after all, he was Jack.

He has reportedly had sex with the mother of the Premier of Canada, Justin Trudeau. As well as with Lara Flynn Boyle, Michelle Phillips, Anjelica Huston, Melanie Griffith, Veronica Cartwright, on and on the list goes. Cher once remarked, "I think he likes women more than any man

I've ever known. I mean he really likes them." A Playboy model once said, "He's a non-stop sex machine." And that he apparently ate peanut butter in bed, between rounds, to keep his stamina going. Kim Bassinger described Jack as, "the most highly sexualized individual I have ever met."

It was rumored that Nicholson spent over $75,000 on a set of made-to-order golf clubs made with carbon fabric, platinum, and 24-karat gold. President Trump is also rumored to own a set as well. But now at age 80, having lived a lavish and debaucherous lifestyle, he's living quite alone. The program ended with Jack telling an interviewer that was afraid of dying alone in his house. It made Edward sad.

Edward turned the program off while thinking to himself, "I know what you mean, Jack."

———◇———

Edward went to bed thinking about Jack Nicholson but hoping he'd dream about Sylvia. However, he couldn't force lustful thoughts into his mind. For some warped reason, he started thinking about Dink. How Dink had become a close friend now, without Edward realizing it. Edward had made friends throughout the years. Some stayed in his life, others came and went—the nature of life. Then there are the people who are always there to lend a helping hand whenever you need it.

As with Dink, some friends have a special bonding. With them, there seems to be no difference between friends and family. Sometimes, friends are closer than family . . . not by blood, but by heart. Everyone wants friends to be in their life forever. To take a genuine interest in them. To be a giver, not a taker. To be loyal. To be a positive person. Someone you can build on common interests. Someone who is open, honest, and real.

Edward wanted someone who was not judgmental and didn't judge him on his past decisions—right or wrong. Someone who was straightforward, someone he could trust and depend on easily. Someone like Dink, or Sylvia maybe. A best friend is someone who knows you like no one else in the world. Someone you can't hide anything from. Someone who cheers you up, who makes you laugh—friends add happiness to your life!

Edward wanted someone who would listen to him on those sad and gloomy days when he was feeling low. Someone he could share his thoughts with, someone he could trust. Someone who would be honest with him, or have empathy to understand what he was experiencing. Someone he could trust with his secrets and his deep thoughts. Someone who would always have his back. He thought a few more seconds, then starting quietly singing an old Carol King song from his youth, or was it James Taylor? He couldn't remember . . . but he could remember the words:

> You just call out my name
> And you know wherever I am
> I'll come running to see you again
> Winter, spring, summer or fall
> All you have to do is call
> And I'll be there
> Yes I will
> You've got a friend.

Edward had sweet dreams. Not of Sylvia, but of being happy. When he awoke, he was unsure exactly what the happiness was in his dream, but he was certain it was there. He took a shower, got a bowl of Frosted Flakes, and sat to watch the morning news before work. Today was apparently the day in history that Archduke Franz Ferdinand and his wife Sophie of Austria were assassinated back in 1914. The killings sparked the chain of events that led to the outbreak of World War 1.

They were both visiting the Bosnian capital of Sarajevo to inspect the imperial forces in Bosnia. The annexation of this land had angered Serbian nationalists, who wanted this territory to be a part of Serbia—not Bosnia. A group of young nationalists hatched a plot to kill the Archduke during his visit. They learned of the parade route through the city and had their plot all planned out.

But, as quite often happens with hot-headed 19-year olds, they got confused and lost and never found the parade with the Archduke. They finally gave up and decided to go back home and think up another plan. They cut through an alley, back to their hotel, only to discover the parade coming down the street as they exited the alley. One of the 19-year olds ran right up the open-topped car carrying the Archduke and his wife and shot them both at point-blank range.

Austria-Hungary declared war on Serbia, and the fragile peace between Europe's great powers collapsed, beginning the conflict known as the Great War, to end all wars. Brought about because a group of hot-headed teenagers who got lost and stumbled out of an alleyway—into history.

Edward was stunned. He'd never heard that story before. He'd let his Frosted Flakes get soggy, but he didn't care. He couldn't wait to tell Dink this story later today.

After work, he hurried to visit Dink and found him at the lake, left of the middle. He sat down and started telling him the story he heard on TV of Archduke Ferdinand. Dink sat there quietly while Edward retold the entire saga. When Edward finished, he smiled and looked at Dink, who replied, "I already knew that."

Edward had a puzzled look on his face and answered, "How could you know it?"

Dink snarled, "How could you NOT know it?"

18

THE NEXT DAY, VISITING DINK, Edward was peppered with all sorts of questions about Sylvia and their relationship. He adroitly avoided every question. Dink would ask, "How often are you seeing Sylvia these days?"

Instead of sitting right next to Dink, Edward sat one space away from him so he could hide his iPhone in his hand, which had some trivia information on the screen. When Dink asked his first question, Edward replied, "The company Amazon, has a warehouse that is the size of 17 American football fields."

Dink looked at him rather querulously and asked, "Does she ever stay over at your house?"

"I read once that President Richard Nixon was an accomplished musician who could play the piano, accordion, violin, saxophone, and clarinet." Dink leaned forward and stared at Edward, who continued, "And, did you know that an American gymnast named George Eyser, competed during the 1904 Summer Games despite having a wooden left leg, and won the gold medals in the vault, parallel bars, and rope climbing?"

Dink then asked, "Well, are you staying over at her house?"

Edward looked down at his phone and replied, "England is smaller than New York State. And Charlie Chaplin once entered a 'Charlie Chaplin look-alike contest' and came in third."

Dink blurted out, "I asked you a question, Ed!"

Edward responded, "The largest air force in the world is the U.S. Air Force. The second largest air force in the world is the U.S. Navy."

"Ed!"

Edward only responded, "Of all the people in the history of the world that have reached the age of 65, half of them are living right now."

Dink was nonplussed and asked, "Well, you're doing more than kissing her aren't you, son?"

"Dink, did you know that when your mother was born, she was already carrying the egg that would become you?"

"Ed, women need physical attention."

Edward smiled and replied, "The Bible has been translated into Klingon, the alien language used in Star Trek."

"Women like to be touched and caressed, Ed."

"Female kangaroos have three vaginas."

That news seemed to temporarily amaze Dink. His mouth dropped open a little and he squinted his eyes, so Edward continued, "The average person in the U.S. spends two weeks of their life watching a traffic light change. And Dink, the percentage of American men who say they would marry the same woman if they had it to do all over again is 80%. But the percentage of American women who say they would marry the same man is only 50%.

And Dink, did you know that the only animal besides a human that can get sunburned is a pig?"

Dink suddenly stood up and started shuffling away without a word. He shuffled two or three times before he realized he forgot his cane. He turned to go back for it, but Edward was standing right behind him and handed it to him. Dink snatched it from Edward's hand and returned to his shuffle up the sidewalk, only slowing down to look for pennies here and there.

———

Edward and Sylvia had not, in fact, stayed over with each other. However, Edward was aware that Sylvia liked to be touched. He was even getting used to the illogical banter Sylvia spouted out as Edward began to arouse her. As Edward would kiss her, then begin rubbing her back and arm, Sylvia would suddenly spurt out things like, "Walt Disney dropped out of high school at 16. And originally named Mickey Mouse, Mortimer Mouse, but his wife made him change it because it sounded too pompous. He measured distance in hotdogs. Trash cans at Disney World were placed 25 steps away from hot dog stands since that was how long it took him to eat a hot dog."

At first, these inane trivialities made Edward wonder if Sylvia was enjoying the fruits of his labor. But, as her breaths grew shorter and her pulse grew quicker, he soon learned to ignore the trivial blabber, such as, "Edward, George Washington died after his doctors removed 40% of his blood, over 80 ounces, during a 12-hour period to cure a throat infection." Then, several more heavy breaths, "He once stopped a battle during the Revolutionary War to return a lost dog to the enemy." Heart racing. "When he died, Napoleon ordered ten days of mourning in France."

Edward began rubbing in a more sensitive area as she continued, "When he was elected President, no one knew what to call him. No other nation had ever elected a president." Extreme heavy breathing, "He wrote between 18,000 and 20,000 letters during his lifetime, but when he died, his wife burned most of them. And, his teeth weren't made of wood, Edward. They were made of gold, ivory, lead, human, and animal teeth. After his presidency, he became a whiskey tycoon and owned the largest distillery in the U.S."

Sylvia could hardly breathe as she finally spouted out, "There are 189 things named after George Washington: 1 state, 7 mountains, 8 streams, 10 lakes, 33 counties, 9 colleges, and 121 towns and villagesssssssssss." Edward then thrust his tongue deep into Sylvia's open mouth, half because he was desperately in the throes of romance, and half just to hopefully shut her up.

Later, after things had significantly cooled off, Edward excitedly remarked, "Wow! That was out of this world!"

Sylvia replied, "Edward, sex is banned aboard the International Space Station. And space is only sixty-two miles above sea level."

Edward said, "Sixty-two miles you say?"

"Yes. And, without space suits, humans could only live for about thirty seconds in space. In 1977 we received a signal from deep space that lasted 72 seconds. We still don't know how or where it came from. And astronauts aboard Apollo 10 heard unexplained 'outer spacey' music while orbiting the dark side of the moon. Maybe that's where Led Zepplin got the idea for that album."

Edward quickly corrected her, "It wasn't Led Zepplin, it was Pink Floyd."

"And here's something weird, Edward, cockroaches raised in space become quicker, stronger, faster, and tougher than cockroaches on Earth. And this still makes me sad today, Edward . . . the astronauts in the Challenger disaster survived the initial explosion and were alive for nearly three minutes until the cabin crashed into the ocean at a speed of 200 mph."

They were both silent a few moments until Edward said, "I read that if you could see as well as the camera on the Hubble Space Telescope, you would be able to read the fine print on a newspaper at one mile away."

Sylvia pulled back a bit to look directly into Edward's eyes and said, "Edward, we're talking about astronaut's lives here. Have some respect!"

19

"ED, DID YOU JUST CALL ME?"

"No, Dink, I didn't call you. Why?"

"Well, my phone rang and I thought it might've been you telling me you were coming over. But I guess not."

"Do you want me to come over, Dink?"

"Do what you want to do! I'm not begging anybody to come over here. You're a grown man. You can make your own decisions. Bye!"

Edward went over. He found Dink in the reception area drinking a glass of white wine. As soon as he sat down, without any introduction, Dink said, "Do you remember John F. Kennedy, Ed?"

"Yeah, Dink. Everybody remembers JFK."

"He was a good man. He gave his entire salary from the Presidency to charity every year. And he was the first President to dance with African American women at an inauguration ball."

Edward said, "Yeah, I think I remember hearing that."

"Well, I bet you don't know that before he was killed, that he survived four assassination attempts, did you?"

"What?" Edward had indeed not heard this.

"Yes, a retired postal worker attempted to kill him barely a month after the election. He followed him from Hyannis Port, Mass. To Georgetown, near Washington, DC to Palm Beach, Florida in a car loaded with dynamite. Other plots in Chicago and Tampa were discovered in the weeks before November 22, 1963.

"He was a cursed man, Ed. He received Last Rites four times in his life. He first received them in 1947 after becoming gravely ill in England, and next received them in 1951 when he got a severe fever in Japan. And he got them again in 1954 after back surgery and lastly on that bleak day in November."

Edward was enthralled and waited for Dink to continue after he took a healthy drink from his wine glass.

"He was an avid fan of 'James Bond' and he wrote his own spy novel about a coup d'état organized by Vice President Lyndon Johnson. The day before he ordered the ban on Cuban imports, he bought 1,200 high-grade Cuban cigars. He just wasn't a healthy man, Ed. He suffered from Addison's disease, which was potentially fatal in the 1960's. He also suffered from colitis, prostatitis, and osteoporosis of the lower back. That was why he didn't slump over in his car the day he was shot. The back brace he was wearing prevented him from slumping over. If he had slumped over after the first shot, he wouldn't have taken that fatal shot to the head."

Dink took another drink of wine. Edward wished he had a glass of wine. They were both saddened by these facts. And they both sat there reminiscing about Camelot and what could have been.

Dink signaled for one of the staff to bring Edward a glass of wine. He didn't ask Edward what sort of wine he wanted, or even if he wanted a glass of wine. As one of the staff once described Dink, "When he goes to Spain, HE chases the bulls." So, if Dink ordered you a glass of wine—you drank it.

As soon as the waiter left, Dink continued his monologue, "Princess Diana was another sad story, Ed. Do you remember her? She married into the Royal family, and . . ."

"Yes, Dink, I remember her."

"Well, her wedding in 1981 was broadcast in 74 countries and watched by 750 million people worldwide. Her funeral, 16 years later, had 2.5 billion viewers. When she first met Charles, Prince of Wales, in 1977, he was dating her sister at the time. Diana was involved in swimming and diving and studying ballet and tap dance. That's how old Charles noticed her. But the age difference between them, 13 years, was just too much to overcome. Charles wanted a more matronly wife and she wanted more life in her husband. It was sad. Within five years of marriage, it all started unraveling.

At the divorce, she received a lump sum settlement of 17 million euros, as well as 400,000 Euros per year. In 1997, she was involved in that fatal car crash in Paris that killed her, her boyfriend, and the chauffeur. But what was not made public, Ed was that she wasn't removed from the wrecked car for almost 37 minutes—despite there being little to no damage to her side of the car. In fact, it was a total of 81 minutes before the ambulance arrived.

When the ambulance finally came and left the scene of the crash on its way to the hospital, it traveled at only 12 mph. This was later questioned by investigators, and the reason given for the slowness was the ambulance had high-tech medical equipment on board and they had begun treatment on Diana and to travel at high speed would have put this delicate work in danger.

The actual collision between the Mercedes, carrying Diana, and a white Fiat has also been questioned. Suspicions grew when the white Fiat that hit Diana's car was never officially located despite a nationwide search. It appeared to have vanished into thin air."

Edward was waiting for more, he wanted more, but that was the end of Dink's story. Dink sat there nodding to himself, thinking abstract, imperceptible, and transcendent thoughts. Edward was wondering what this ill tasting wine was and what Sylvia might be doing later tonight.

Sylvia was watching a television special on billionaires. It fascinated her. The first person in the series was the writer of the "Harry Potter" books, J.K. Rowling. Before she published her first book, she was a single mother living on welfare. Some five years later she became a billionaire! Her seven books have sold 450 million copies and the movies have brought in $7.7 billion on their own. Sylvia became lost in a daydream . . . she could write her own book. She could tell her own story. She could become famous and rich . . . she could do it. Her inner voice was very convincing. All she had to do was—do it!

The next billionaire was someone Sylvia had never heard of—John Fredriksen. He was Norway's richest man until he defected to Cyprus in the mid-1990's to avoid taxes. However, he lives most of the year in a $172 million estate in London. He controls the largest fleet of supertankers in the world. He was a high school dropout who made his entire fortune on his own—unlike many who inherited their wealth. He is entirely old school and shuns computers and is fond of wearing a cravat. He insists on reading everything on paper and personally maintains records on all his companies in 19 suitcases, which he is constantly rummaging through to discern patterns that will help him in his tanker business.

Sylvia was enthralled and ran to the refrigerator to grab a glass of tomato juice before the next segment, which was about "Count Dracula," Ion Tiriac. Tiriac was a former pro tennis and ice hockey star. He speaks nine languages and has been known to eat six steaks, four plates of pasta, and twelve eggs just for breakfast! One writer once wrote that Tiriac has been to places that most people do not imagine exist. He's known for his deadpan humor and expressionless face, which he hides under a massive mustache. It's said that few people have ever seen him smile.

He was an Olympic ice hockey player for Romania before switching to tennis, where he won the men's doubles title at the 1970 French Open. He made his fortune after his playing career, founding Romania's first post-communist bank in 1990, which he named after himself. He then got into retail, insurance, autos, and airlines in his home country. And he even appeared in a Miller Lite commercial in 1987 with legendary baseball personality Bob Uecker. How and where he spends his money these days is known only to the mystical Tiriac himself.

Sylvia's phone then rang. She noticed it was from Edward and she thought about answering it—almost. But the next billionaire was a woman, and Sylvia didn't want to miss her story. China, the world's most populous nation, also has more female billionaires than any other country. 60% of the world's women billionaires are from China. A good number of them are also millennials, including Wu Yan. They call her the "media and entertainment queen." And at 36 years of age, she is also the youngest of China's self-made billionaires.

What's really crazy about Yan's wealth is that she started her career as a journalist, which is traditionally a low-paying career choice. But Yan pivoted into entertainment and became chairwoman of tech giant

Hakim Unique before it went public. This company produces television shows and movies, runs theme parks and theater, creates video games, and also has built smart cities—all under Yan's guidance.

Perhaps the world's stingiest billionaire is Ingvar Kamprad, who founded the furniture brand IKEA at the ripe age of 17. He is known to shun life at every turn. He flies economy class and stays at budget hotels—where he'd rather replace a minibar soda himself than pay the marked-up hospitality price. He rides the subway and drives an old Volvo, and he's even published several works detailing his frugality and how it coincides with the IKEA approach to business and interior design. However, he admitted that IKEA was the biggest mistake of his life. All he ever wanted was a simple life and to be left alone.

Sylvia finished her tomato juice as the last billionaire was being introduced. This self-proclaimed "Number One King of All Fun" is the epitome of an oddball billionaire. He is the obnoxious and overbearing Stewart Rahr. He likes to call himself Rah Rah and made his money in pharmaceuticals. He boasts of his conquests and exploits via email to all his friends and associates—he likes to brag. Some of these emails include pictures of naked women, or nearly naked women, partying with Rah Rah and various celebrities. In 2012 he was sent to a psychiatric clinic after allegedly pulling a gun on an elevator at Trump Tower in Manhattan.

Sylvia sat mesmerized by this segment. Eventually, she remembered Edward's phone call. She knew what he wanted . . . which was probably the same thing she wanted. She called him right back.

20

TWO DAYS LATER EDWARD STOPPED IN to visit Dink after work. As usual, he was out by the lake—left of the middle. Edward had learned not to say anything upon his arrival, just to sit down and wait . . . Dink would start. And he did.

"Ed, how did the Aborigine's get in Australia?"

The question was so odd, even for Dink, that Edward wasn't certain he heard it correctly, so he said, "What?"

"How did they get there? That question has been bothering me for some time now. Think about, Ed. How did they get there?"

Edward nodded his head and tried to look as though he knew how to answer that odd question—but he had no clue what to say. Finally, he said, "I guess they evolved there like humans evolved everywhere. Didn't they?"

Dink turned his entire body towards Edward and asked, "So you believe in evolution, do you, Ed?"

"Well . . . don't you, Dink?"

"I'm asking you, Ed. Do you believe it or not?"

Edward was quite certain that whichever answer he gave Dink would be met with an inquisitive furor. So, selfishly and defensively, he remained quiet. Dink looked sternly at him and asked another question, "Do you believe in God, Ed? Do you believe He spoke everything into existence? Or, do you believe we all evolved from apes? Well, most of us anyway . . . some so-called people I know have never made that transition."

Edward thought to himself, "There is no way in the world I'm going to answer these questions. Just stay still, be quiet, and maybe he'll move on to another subject." He was wrong.

"Well, Ed? How did they get there?"

Edward stared out into the lake and wondered what Sylvia might be wearing later tonight when he stopped by her house.

Dink was not going to let this pass, "You know, Ed, Australia is the only continent that is an island. It always has been. It's never been connected to any other land mass. So the often used theory that people walked there like they did across the so-called land bridge to North America, or to South America, or to Africa, just doesn't make sense. So, how did they get there?"

Edward was hoping Sylvia would be wearing something loose and provocative.

"They've found skeletons there, Ed, that carbon dating concludes are over 40,000 years old. Do you believe that?"

Or, maybe she could be wearing that blouse she likes that is very low cut in front.

"Ed, Australia is in the middle of the ocean. There is only one piece of land within a hundred miles of it, and the ocean is rough through that stretch with currents and tides making it nearly impossible to navigate with the best of equipment. Humans only learned how to make navigable boats about three or four thousand years ago. How did these Aborigines get there 40,000 years ago? I don't understand it, Ed."

Edward awoke from his Sylvia dream and answered, "Well, I guess they must've built some kind of boat, Dink."

"Ed, did you not hear what I just told you? The technology to build a boat that would sail the ocean wasn't available to them 40,000 years ago. Plus, think about it, Ed . . . the people in Indonesia didn't know Australia was there. So you think some pre-historic men, unfathomably just built a boat and started sailing out into the ocean without knowing where they're going? Really, Ed? And even if they did, do you think they took women with them? No, of course not."

"Well, Dink, they must have."

"Ed, when the English finally came to Australia in the early 1800's and found the Aborigines, they had nothing! No houses, no tools, no shelters, no clothes, no farming, no domesticated animals, no pottery—NOTHING! They completely lived off the land and what they could find. There has never been any archeological evidence of anything from them. No ruins, no earthworks, no artwork, no nothing. So now you think these people who had absolutely nothing in 1800, somehow managed to build a boat, 40,000 years ago, and sail into the unknown sea, not knowing where they were going, and land in Australia? Really, Ed?"

Edward cracked his knuckles and spit on the ground, but never even tried to answer that question.

"So I ask you again, Ed . . . how did they get there? There have never been any monkeys in Australia for men to evolve from. No evidence anywhere on the entire continent of any apes ever living there. No evidence of pre-historic, or Cro-magnum, or anything. Just the Aborigines as they are now—the same now as they were 40,000 years ago. So, how did they get there, Ed? How?"

Edward thought briefly about that question, then started wondering if Sylvia would make some Fuzzy Navels for them tonight. He liked Fuzzy Navels.

Edward was finally able to make an exit. Dink seemed not to notice his absence as he continued to ponder that unanswerable question he had thought about all day. Edward went to Sylvia's house to find her dressed in some old blue jeans and a sweatshirt as she was cleaning her house. Edward was a little disappointed. She offered him some sweet tea, which he gladly took, and as he tasted it, he asked her, "Sylvia, how did the Aborigines get in Australia?"

Sylvia immediately stopped what she was doing and answered, "God put them there, Edward. How else do you think they could've gotten there?" And she went back to dusting and cleaning and vacuuming, while Edward pondered that question and answer, and wondered why he couldn't have said that same thing to Dink.

21

DINK HAD ANOTHER DOCTOR'S VISIT and when he returned he was unusually quiet. Edward told him he'd be waiting on him and expected the full barrage of medical trivia from Dink. Instead, he got nothing. Edward asked him if he wanted to go out by the lake, but Dink only wanted to sit down and have a glass of wine. They sat in silence for about half a glass, then Dink began his soliloquy.

"Ed, did you know that an ordinary pencil has the potential to draw a line 38 miles long."

"I didn't know that, Dink. How did your doctor's visit go? Is everything alright?"

"And if a man never cut his beard, by the time he dies it would be 30 feet long."

Edward didn't respond, but he did slap his arm at a mosquito who had bitten him. Dink noticed and said, "A mosquito has 47 teeth." Edward looked over at Dink . . . and Dink nodded. Then added, "Nowhere in the Humpty Dumpty Nursery Rhyme does it say that Humpty Dumpty is an egg. Isn't that odd? And in 2007, an American man tried to fake his own death in order to get out of his cell phone contract without paying a fee. It didn't work. Death, Ed, always wins."

That was an ominous statement to make just after your doctor's visit. Edward stared at Dink, who then added, "People always think they'll face death very bravely, but most of us won't. We're mostly sniveling cowards. But not Donald Ballard, Ed. He was not a coward. He won the Medal of Honor when he jumped on a live grenade to save his buddies. In Vietnam, he was helping with some wounded men when a Vietcong soldier threw a grenade amongst them. Ballard leaped over a stretcher and pulled the grenade under his body. The grenade did not go off. But for his selfless act of courage, he won the Medal of Honor. Would you have done that, Ed?" Before Edward could answer, Dink added, "I probably wouldn't have."

"Dink, did you get bad news from the doctor today?" Dink didn't answer right away. He took a couple of sips from his wine glass, then said,

"I'm fine, Ed, but let me tell you about bad luck." Edward hadn't mentioned 'bad luck,' he asked Dink about any 'bad news.' But that didn't deter Dink from his story, "There was an English couple on vacation in New York when the terrorists attacked on 9/11. Four years later, this same couple happened to be in London during the worst terror attack in their history, when a series of bombs exploded across the city's transit system, killing 52 people. Then, three years later they took another vacation to the exotic Indian city of Mumbai where they saw the worst terror attack in that country's history, as shooting and bombing attacks killed and wounded hundreds. That's bad luck, Ed. Not some prognosis from a backwater doctor."

"Did the doctor tell you something you didn't like?"

"Ed, why don't you and Sylvia come and have dinner with me tomorrow night? My treat. They're having prime rib. I bet Sylvia likes prime rib, doesn't she?"

"I don't know if she does or not, Dink. But I'll ask her."

Sylvia did indeed like prime rib, but she was even more so looking forward to sparing with Dink again. Dink was waiting outside the Arbor Room dining hall when they arrived and greeted them warmly. Sylvia said, "Very nice to see you again, Mr. Cleveland. I've been looking forward to it."

Dink smiled and said, "Please, Sylvia, call me Dink."

Sylvia smiled back, at least it looked like a smile, and replied, "So, Mr. Cleveland, you say the prime rib here is good?"

"It's supposed to be, Sylvia, although I've never tasted it myself. I'm a bit leery of cows nowadays since I learned that they now produce four times as much milk as they did fifty years ago."

Sylvia then exclaimed, "It didn't seem to bother Charles Darwin much. He ate every animal he discovered."

Dink bit, "The deadliest animal in Africa is the hippopotamus. Did he eat one of those?"

"He didn't discover the hippopotamus, Mr. Cleveland . . . as you well know. But an animal IS killed for food every one and a half seconds. And the average meat-eating person eats about 7,000 animals in their lifetime."

"Well, humans didn't kill them all, Sylvia. Many animals have been reported to commit suicide, Including dogs, cows, bulls, and sheep."

"That doesn't surprise me, Mr. Cleveland. Animals know. Most mammals, from elephants to shrews, live for the same number of heartbeats, about 1.5 billion, before dying. They instinctively know."

Edward quickly got out his iPhone and found the calculator option, he thought to himself, "Okay 70 beats per minute times 60 minutes equals 4,200 beats per hour, times 24 hours equals 100,800 beats per day, divided into 1.5 billion"---but his iPhone calculator wouldn't compute billions. This temporarily worried Edward.

Dink said, "Ed, did you know that opossums have fifty razor-sharp teeth, the highest number of teeth found in any land mammal?"

Edward knew Dink wasn't talking to him, because he looking directly at Sylvia, who then remarked, "Edward, grizzly bears have the biting capacity enough to crush a bowling ball. And, 70% of all animals in the jungle rely on figs for their survival."

Dink leaned forward, looking straight through Sylvia and said, "A lion can mate almost fifty times in a single day, Ed. And a snail can sleep up to three years continuously."

Not to be outdone, Sylvia added, "Well, the loudest howler monkeys have the tiniest testicles. And, ostriches can run faster than horses, and elephants can smell water three miles away—fascinating, isn't it Edward?"

"Well, Ed, have you ever wondered why birds always veer to the right? While bats always veer to the left, when they come out of their caves?"

No, Edward had never wondered about that. He was still trying to comprehend Sylvia's last statement about the howler monkeys and small testicles . . . and wondering what she really meant by that. Fortunately, the waiter arrived and asked for drink orders, bringing some semblance of sanity to the table.

The dinner was ordered, Sylvia did not get the prime rib. The conversation was "interesting," and everything seemed fairly normal until Sylvia slipped her shoe off and started rubbing her foot up and down Edward's leg. Edward broke out in tiny beads of sweat as he tried to eat his key lime pie without getting choked on it.

Just then, a waiter came to the table to refill the water glasses and spoke to Dink, saying, "You were right about Calamity Jane, Mr. Cleveland. I looked her up and everything you said was true. How do you know all that stuff?"

Dink smiled at the waiter as he walked away, and Edward took the bait, "What was that about, Dink?"

"Aww . . . he saw some western on TV that had Calamity Jane in it and he thought she wasn't a real person—so I had to enlighten him."

Sylvia immediately stopped rubbing Edward's leg as Edward replied, "I didn't think she was real either."

Dink took a sip of sweet tea and said, "Of course she was real, they couldn't make up somebody like her, Ed. About 1865, she moved out to Montana with her family when she was about thirteen years old. She grew up tall and strong and liked to wear men's clothing, and spend her time around men. Like many frontier women, Jane learned to ride and shoot at an early age. She eventually settled in the rugged boomtown of Deadwood, South Dakota. She lost what beauty she may have had, due to the high plains, wind, and sun, her skin was tanned and leathery. She looked more masculine due to her muscular body.

Old Jane was given to hard drinking and carousing, she attracted public attention with stunts like riding a bull down the main street in town. By the late 1890's, Jane's hard living had begun to take a toll, and she was suffering from the debilitating effects of severe alcoholism. But she still traveled around in Wild West shows doing stunts and performing—riding horses, bulls, and doing shooting tricks.

Two years before she died, she seems to have finally tired of living the self-created persona of Calamity Jane. She was found sick and drunk in an African-American bordello in a small town in Montana. She told those who found her to leave her alone, she just wanted to go her own way. She died at the age of 51 in a small South Dakota town."

When Dink finished his story, he looked over at Sylvia, half-way smiled, and pushed his chair back to get up from the table. When he rose, he looked at them both and said,

Gary Hope

"I'm going to bed, you two carry on with whatever it is you're doing under the table. Goodnight."

22

"DINK, HOW DID YOU KNOW ABOUT CALAMITY JANE? Did you live out west in your earlier life?"

"Ed, I didn't so much live in various places, but I stayed with friends all over the country for different lengths of time. America is a great and fascinating country, Ed. You don't need to be a missionary and live in Korea to experience great, beautiful, and wondrous things."

"Uh, oh." Edward thought, "Here we go . . ."

"Ed, did you know that there are more single people than married people in the U.S. nowadays? And, that there are 100 divorces every hour in the U.S.? That's a sad fact, Ed."

"Yeah, it's pretty depressing, Dink. That and all the homelessness in our country. Every corner you see the homeless people out begging for money."

"Let me tell you something, Ed . . . empty homes outnumber the homeless 6 to 1 in the United States. The problem isn't that there aren't enough places for people to live, the problem is that 76% of Americans live paycheck-to-paycheck, and when something bad happens, they have no place to turn. That's why about 20 million Americans live in mobile homes, Ed. It's not that there's no place to live, heck, 47% of the U.S. remains unoccupied, despite us having a population of over 310 million people!"

Edward nodded, he didn't know why he nodded, it just seemed like the thing to do. Then he sighed and said, "Yeah, we always think our country is so rich, but I guess we're not."

"Ed, there's plenty of money, but there's also plenty of stupidity and laziness. 1 in 4 Americans did not read a book last year. Can you believe that? And 63% of all the people in prison can't read at all. And think about this, there are over 9 million people around the world in prison—one-quarter of them are in the U.S. Why is that, Ed? Does America have more criminals than other countries? Or, are we just better at catching them?

Ed, when I went to college it wasn't expensive at all, but now, it costs $245,000 to raise a child, BEFORE they even get to college! It's not that our country has to change, Ed, but somehow the American people have to change. Heck, by the time an average child leaves school now, he has seen over 40,000 murders on TV. They think nothing of it. Ed, I read that 7% of Americans claim they never bathe!"

Edward added, "Well, I know there's a water shortage in some places."

"That's hogwash, Ed! The U.S. uses less water now than it did in 1970. It's not lack of water, its lack of common sense. In the U.S. there are 115,000 janitors, 83,000 bartenders, and 323,000 restaurant servers with bachelor's degrees. And to top that off, it's estimated that more than half of all people claiming to have a new Ph.D. in the U.S. actually have a fake one."

Edward was waiting for the appropriate time to tell Dink of a fact he came across . . . now seemed like the time, "I read that 8 billion chickens are consumed in the U.S. each year."

"Ed, what in the world has that got to do with what we're talking about here? There are places in our country where there are still cases of bubonic plague reported each year, and you're bringing up chickens?"

"Well . . ." Edward didn't how to finish that thought.

"Ed, 97% of rapists in the U.S. never spend a day in jail for their crime. Apple has more operating cash than the U.S. Treasury. More soldiers committed suicide last year than died in combat in 2012, and now the marijuana market in the U.S. is bigger than craft beer, wine, and organic foods—and you're telling me about chickens?"

Edward didn't know how to defend himself, so he picked up a magazine from the table and read the caption, "Hmm, says here the U.S. has 19 aircraft carriers, compared to the rest of world's 12 aircraft carriers. Makes you proud to be an American, doesn't it, Dink?"

"Ed, there are also 4,746 people in our country with an identical first and last name. Does that also make you proud to be an American?"

Edward asked, "The same names? Really?"

"Yes, Thomas Thomas is the most common. Crazy parents couldn't even think of an original name for the own children. I need a drink. Pour us a glass of wine, Ed."

———◇———

Dink enjoyed his glass of wine. Edward didn't like his at all. It tasted like turpentine and paint thinner, mixed with tomato juice . . . but he would never tell Dink that. When Dink finished his glass of wine, he poured another one and said, "Ed, I'm going to give you a geography lesson."

Edward thought to himself, "Uh, oh, I'm supposed to be at Sylvia's house in about an hour."

"On France's southern Mediterranean coast, Cannes, the sunny summer playground of the rich, which is sometimes incorrectly called 'tropical,' is about 10 miles farther NORTH than Milwaukee, Wisconsin. And the little town of Estcourt Station, Maine, which is the northernmost tip of Maine, is still 300 miles farther SOUTH than London, England. That's how geography is, Ed . . . it can fool you.

And speaking England, the entire country, with over 50 million residents, is smaller than the state of Louisiana. And guess what, Ed . . . the biggest pyramid in the world is NOT in Egypt—it's in Mexico. Have you ever been to Los Angeles, Ed?"

Before Edward could answer, Dink continued, "As you know it's on the Pacific Ocean, but Reno, Nevada, being over 300 miles from the ocean, is farther west than Los Angeles." Edward didn't really believe that and made a mental note to check his computer when he got back home.

"China and Russia are each bordered by 14 countries . . . 14, Ed! And Africa is the only continent that is in all four hemispheres: north, south, east, and west. Whereas, the state of Alaska is both the westernmost and easternmost state in our country."

Dink took a long sip of wine and continued, "What do you know about Russia, Ed?" Edward knew little about

Russia, but he did know better than to interrupt Dink when he was on a roll, especially if he was going to make it to Sylvia's house on time. "77% of Russia is made up of Siberia. And in Russia, there are 9 million more women than men—think about that, Ed. Over there, beer was not even considered an alcoholic beverage until 2013. They have over 500,000 alcohol-related deaths each year.

25% of Russians die before reaching the age of 55, compared to just 1% in the U.S.—Vodka is to blame. School teachers over there can be paid in vodka, if they wish. Ed, Apple Corp is worth more than the entire Russian stock market. And they did a survey which showed that a third of all Russians believe the sun revolves around the earth. They have over 800,000 faith healers, but only 640,000 doctors. Texas, New York, and California all have economies bigger than Russia."

Edward finally spoke and asked, "Then why does everyone fear the Russians so much, Dink?"

"Because, Ed, Russia has over 8,400 nuclear weapons, more than any other country. And you can't trust them. It's believed they have at least 15 secret cities with their names and locations unknown—even to the CIA."

Edward then took a big sip of his ill-tasting wine as he thought about a country full of drunks, hidden cities, and 8,400 nuclear weapons. After a few moments of silence, Dink said, "I'd like to tell you more, Ed, but I don't want you to keep Sylvia waiting."

Edward said, "Okay." And as he started walking for the door, he thought to himself, "Wait a minute . . . I didn't tell him I was meeting Sylvia." He started to ask Dink about that, but his inner voice convinced him to leave while he had the chance.

When Edward arrived at Sylvia's, she had her hair tied up in a towel, letting it dry. Edward asked, "Don't you have a hair dryer?"

"Oh, Edward, sometimes you men amaze me. Don't you want me to look my best?"

"But I thought we were staying in tonight and watching an old movie?"

"Yes, we are! But don't you want me to look good?"

Edward wondered if there was any way in the world to answer that question without getting himself in trouble.

Instead, he said, "I just came from Dink's, he was telling me some stuff about geography."

Sylvia's head turned so quickly that the towel came untied. She quickly rewrapped her hair and replied, "If you wanted to know about geography, Edward, you should've asked me. Just what did you want to know?"

"I didn't want to know anything. You know how it is with Dink, he just starts telling you stuff that's interesting."

Sylvia huffed up and said, "You mean like how all the interstates in America are required to have at least one mile in five be completely straight so they can be used as airstrips in times of war or other emergencies? Or that how India has more people than the United States, Indonesia, Pakistan, and Bangladesh combined?"

Edward totally and completely wished he had never brought up the subject of geography. He didn't say a word, hoping Sylvia wouldn't say any more words . . . no chance of that.

"Or that how the Amazon River pushes so much water into the Atlantic Ocean that, more than one hundred miles at sea off the mouth of the river, one can dip fresh water out of the ocean. And that how the volume of water in the Amazon River is **greater than the next eight largest rivers** in the world combined and three times the flow of all rivers in the United States. That kind of stuff, Edward?"

Poor Edward . . .

"Or how Canada has more lakes than the rest of the world combined? Or maybe he told you about a place In the Sahara Desert where there is a town named **Tidikelt**, which did not receive a drop of rain for **ten years**. Technically though, the driest place on Earth is in the valleys of the Antarctic near Ross Island. There has been no rainfall there for two million years. Did he tell you that, Edward?"

Edward did not answer. Edward was afraid to answer.

"Well? Did he, Edward?"

"Umm . . . no, he didn't, honey. What movie are we watching tonight?"

23

THE MOVIE SYLVIA PICKED OUT wasn't one Edward would have chosen. It was a musical from the 1950's, with old dance tunes and Broadway show songs. After a few minutes, Sylvia began again: "Edward, I was thinking about geography and you know I've lived in many, many places. I don't know why you didn't ask me if you wanted to know anything. Take Utah for example. I lived there with my parents for almost eighteen months. Now, I love the Mormons, but, Edward, they are a strange lot! Did you know that in Salt Lake City it is illegal to walk down the street carrying a paper bag containing a violin?" Before Edward could respond to that weirdness, she continued, "Well, it is. But, Utah has the highest literacy rate in the United States. And, Edward, the Great Salt Lake is about four times saltier than any of the world's oceans. If a person boiled 1 quart of water from this lake, a half a cup of salt would remain."

"A half a cup of salt? Really?"

"Yes, Edward. Do you think I'm joking? I'm not! And even though approximately 62% of Utahans are Mormons, Utah has the highest rate of online porn subscriptions in the United States. And even though polygamy is supposed to be illegal there, it's estimated there are roughly 40,000 polygamous marriages in the state." Sylvia looked over at Edward to make sure he was paying attention. He was, he was paying attention to the top of her blouse which was unbuttoned. So she continued, "And did you know that the U.S. government owns over 2/3 of Utah, Edward?"

Edward did not know that, nor did he care, but he was hoping Sylvia would lean just a little bit more forward. "And, Edward, there is a portion of I-70 in Utah that has a 106-

mile stretch that has no gasoline or any exits. It is the longest such portion in the country. The gas station at the end of this lonely stretch sells about 30 gas containers a week to people who run out on the highway and have to walk to the station. And talking about driving, Edward, more Utahans, died last year from prescription drug overdoses than in car wrecks! And listen to this, Edward . . . there is a stretch of road on I-80 on the salt flats with over a 50-mile straightaway—no curves at all. 50 miles, Edward!"

Edward was pretty sure at this point that Sylvia was not wearing a bra. But she had leaned back on the couch after that last bit of information. So, to get her excited once again, Edward said, "Wow, that sure was interesting, what else do you know, honey?"

"Well . . . you know my parents lived in China once as missionaries. You knew that didn't you, Edward?"

She leaned forward again as Edward answered, "Yes, I remember you telling me that. I bet that was interesting."

"Oh, Edward, you have no idea! China is amazing. 100 million people there live on less than 1 U.S. dollar per day. Think about that! And, over 35 million people there still live in caves. Caves, Edward! China is so full that almost a third of San Francisco's air pollution comes from China." Sylvia was bouncing a little on the couch as she remembered some of these facts. Edward liked bouncing.

"And every 30 seconds a baby is born with a birth defect in China. Also, every year a million girl fetuses and tens of thousands of girl babies are abandoned because of the one-child policy they have. Two years from now, China will have about 40 million men who cannot find wives. And think about this, Edward . . . more people go to church on Sunday in China than in all of Europe. What do you think of that?"

Edward was enjoying China.

"In China, every year, nearly 4 million cats are eaten as a delicacy. And half of all the pigs in the world live in China. Think about that Edward. If a college student gets caught cheating on exams there . . . they can get 7 years in jail for cheating. And guess what else, Edward . . . 1/3 of Chinese women have never heard of tampons, but yet China has 190 Billionaires and 2 million millionaires! But would you live there, Edward? Breathing the air of Beijing has the same health risks as smoking 21 cigarettes a day. And they don't play around there either . . . China executes the death penalty more than 4 times the rest of the world combined. Are you paying attention, Edward?"

Oh, yes. Edward was definitely paying attention to the bouncing and the hopes that the next top button would come loose.

"Edward, one out of every 3 socks you have is made in China. In fact, if Walmart were a country, it would be China's sixth largest export market. And they build a new skyscraper there every 5 days—think about that, Edward!"

Edward was thinking alright. He was thinking really hard how he could somehow loosen that top button and see what the consequences might be.

"Don't you find that fascinating, Edward?"

"Yes, I truly do." And he truly did.

But nothing else happened as Sylvia changed channels and started watching reruns of Jeopardy while answering nearly every question that came up. Edward daydreamed until Final Jeopardy when he surprised Sylvia by knowing the final question when she didn't. "He was a Gold Medal Olympic athlete, a pro football player, he starred in track and field, played baseball and lacrosse, and won a ballroom dancing contest."

Edward blurted out, "Jim Thorpe."

"No, Edward . . . you lose. It's "WHO is Jim Thorpe?"

Sylvia had to win . . . she just had to.

24

"ED, ARE YOU GETTING SERIOUS WITH SYLVIA?"

Edward thought about that question for a few moments, then asked Dink, "Define serious."

"Serious meaning that you're engaging in pre-marital sex with her."

Edward was afraid that's what he meant, "I don't think that's any of your business, Dink. That sort of stuff is personal."

"Well, Sylvia said you were."

"Sylvia told you we were having sex? Why in the world would she tell you that? What we do is our business, she shouldn't be telling people about our personal lives."

"Well, she didn't really tell me . . . but you just did. You need to be careful, Ed. Are you using condoms?"

"Dink!"

"What? I'm just trying to help you and protect you from disease and unwanted pregnancy. What's wrong with that? There are lots of things you probably don't understand about the human body, Ed."

"Like what? How nosy some people can be?"

"No, like that there are 100,000 miles of blood vessels in your body, Ed. And that the strongest muscle in your body is your jaw muscle—did you know that?"

Edward was silent. He wanted to answer, but also didn't want to answer. So Dink continued, "And human bones, ounce for ounce, are stronger than steel. But yet, your bones are composed of 31% water. Pretty interesting isn't it?" Yes, it was, but Edward was still pouting and not answering. "And when you kiss Sylvia, think about this: there are more bacteria in your mouth than there are people in the world." At this fact, Edward turned slightly to look at

Dink, who continued, "Cornflakes have more genes than people do, Ed."

"How can that be?"

"It's true. And all that dust underneath your bed is actually your own dead skin. And by the way, sleeping less than 7 hours a night reduces your life expectancy, Ed." No comment from Edward, but Dink could tell he was interested in these facts, so he continued, "Your nose can remember 50,000 different scents, and your body has enough iron in it to make a metal nail 3 inches long. And, I've noticed you have hazel colored eyes, Ed, which explains your wine drinking habits."

"What difference does the color of my eyes make?"

"Because, Ed, people with blue eyes have a higher alcohol tolerance. And your heartbeat changes and mimics the music you listen to . . . did you know that?"

"No."

"Your brain keeps developing until your late 40's . . . so you've still got time, Ed."

"Time for what?"

"To learn, Ed! Learn that your heart is not on the left side of your body like most people think. It's in the middle. And that without your pinky finger you would lose about 50% of your hand strength. I've noticed you don't have a lot of hair on your arms, Ed. Is your chest hairy?"

"Why in the world would you want to know that, Dink?"

"Because having excessive body hair is linked to a higher intellect, Ed."

"Well, I'm not going to take my shirt off just to satisfy your curiosity, Dink."

"That's okay, Sylvia has already told me you're not that hairy."

"What? She did not. Did she?"

"Ed, when you take one step, you're using up to 200 different muscles."

"Enough, Dink." Edward then turned away from the bench and spat on the ground in disgust.

But Dink couldn't stop, "An average person produces about 25,000 quarts of saliva in a lifetime—enough to fill two swimming pools."

Edward wanted to spit again, but he swallowed instead, then got up and said, "I need a glass of wine. Do you want one?"

"Of course I do, Ed . . . but did you know . . ."

"No more talking, Dink! Only drinking." So they shuffled off to the building—as fast as Dink could shuffle while still looking for pennies. Edward was thinking about his less than hairy chest, while Dink was thinking of a fact he'd recently read, "25 million American adults are living with their parents." And thinking how sad that must be for the parents.

Dink chose a red wine that smelled like three-day-old laundry to Edward. Edward chose something light and sweet. When Edward picked up the two glasses from the waiter, the waiter asked him, "How's Mr. Cleveland doing these days?"

Edward couldn't think of an adequate reply, so he simply said, "You know how he is . . . he doesn't change."

"Yep, if Mr. Cleveland were to punch you in the face you would have to fight off a strong urge to thank him."

Edward didn't exactly agree with that assessment . . . but he didn't disagree with it either.

25

EDWARD AND DINK HAD SETTLED IN the same routine for several weeks: Edward visiting, drinking a glass of wine, denying all inquiries about himself and Sylvia, and listening to Dink spout off all sorts of trivia—some interesting, some bizarre. Edward and Sylvia had also settled into a routine: going out to dinner Saturday nights, watching television together two or three nights a week, and Edward listening to Sylvia's version of trivia. Some interesting and some bizarre. Edward was unaware of the fact that he was acquiring this trivial knowledge through osmosis—even if he didn't want to.

He went to get his three-week haircut and quite innocently started telling the barber about President Franklin Roosevelt. "Russ," the barber's name, "two weeks before FDR was inaugurated for the first time, he arrived in Miami, Florida to give a speech from the back seat of his car. When he finished the speech and was talking to some reporters, five shots rang out. An Italian immigrant, an unemployed bricklayer, had emptied his .32 pistol at FDR. The assassin was only 25 feet away, but his 5'1" height prevented him from seeing clearly. He stood on a wobbly chair but still missed FDR with all five shots. However, four bystanders were hit and the mayor of Chicago was hit in the stomach and died.

FDR remained calm, brave, and decisive during the whole affair. His driver wanted to drive away quickly, but FDR ordered the car to stop and pick up the wounded. He spent several hours at the hospital visiting the wounded and even came back the following day to check on the patients. The assassin said he tried to kill FDR because he blamed him and all rich people and capitalists for his chronic stomach pain. He was found guilty and sentenced to die. He strode to the electric chair and plunked himself down and said, "Pusha da button!"

They did.

Edward turned around in the barber's seat to look at Russ when he finished his story, but Russ was adjusting his earbuds and quietly singing along to the latest Justin Beiber song. Edward was disappointed, but he gave Russ a nice tip just the same.

Edward then stopped at the grocery store to pick up some steaks he and Sylvia were planning on cooking out tomorrow. The butcher was humming an old Beatles' song and Edward asked, "You like the Beatles?"

"Yeah, I guess so. They were pretty good. Here it is fifty years later and people are still singing their songs."

Edward said, "You know Ringo had originally agreed to play another summer with a different band for 20 pounds a week but backed out when John and Paul offered him 25 pounds a week to play with them."

"Really, I never heard that before."

Edward was proud of himself and then said, "Yeah. Poor old Ringo had his appendix almost burst when he was six years old and he fell into a coma for two months. When he finally awoke, he remained in the hospital for several more months. And when he was grown he developed an aptitude for mechanics and could dismantle a car engine and put it back together again without a problem. Pretty weird, huh?"

The poor butcher had heard more than he ever wanted to hear about Ringo, but Edward didn't stop, "People think Ringo wasn't as talented as the others but had nearly perfect tempo. The Beatles would record a song 50 or 60 times, trying to edit together the different parts to get the best possible version. Today, a metronome is used for this same purpose, but the Beatles depended on Ringo to keep the tempo consistent. Had he not had this ability, the Beatles recordings would sound completely different today."

The butcher was nodding while backing slowly towards the storeroom. As he made his getaway, another hapless customer came near Edward, who turned to him and continued, "In 1980 Ringo crashed his Mercedes, carrying his girlfriend, Barbara Bach, in the passenger seat. After the near-fatal accident, the two vowed to never be apart again. They married and are still together. Later that year, when John Lennon was killed, Ringo and his wife went to visit Yoko Ono. When Yoko insisted that she only wanted to see Ringo, Ringo retorted, 'Look, it was you who started all this. We're both coming in.' Yoko relented."

The unwitting customer said, "I just wanted some pork chops." Edward finally got his steaks but wondered why the other customer left without their pork chops. That was certainly strange. When Edward had crossed the parking lot his phone rang. It was Dink.

"Hello, Dink."

"How did you know it was me?"

"Lucky guess, plus my phone has caller ID."

"Oh . . . did you just call me, Ed?"

"No, Dink, I've been shopping."

"Shopping for what?"

This could be delicate. Should he tell Dink that he and Sylvia were planning to grill out steaks? Would Dink want to come? Would it hurt his feelings that he wasn't invited? Hmm. However, before Edward could decide what to say, Dink continued, "I forgot to tell you, I only like sirloins. You and Sylvia can eat whatever you like at the cookout, but I only eat sirloins. You got that?"

"Yeah, I got it. How did you know about the cookout? I was just getting ready to call you and ask if you could come." He lied.

"How do you think I knew about it, Sylvia told me. Sirloins, Ed. Remember that!" And Dink ended the call. Edward stared at his phone for a few seconds, then turned around to go back into the grocery store to buy Dink a sirloin. He thought about calling Sylvia to ask why she invited Dink to their cookout . . . but changed his mind.

At the cookout, Sylvia, Edward, and Dink sat outside under a zelkova tree and had a glass of red wine while the steaks cooked. Edward secretly poured half of his on the ground when no one was looking. The subject of travel came up and Sylvia started telling them about a trip to Ireland she and her best friend had taken two years ago.

"Ireland?" Dink huffed. Who in their right mind would want to go there?"

Sylvia said, "The castles alone make it interesting, Mr. Cleveland."

"Castles? They're all ugly. You've seen one, you've seen them all."

Sylvia said, "The locals on some of the islands still speak the Irish language and knit their own sweaters."

"Big deal! They're all too busy drinking to do much else anyway."

Sylvia volunteered, "The cliffs along the Ring of Kerry are breathtaking."

"Skip it. You've seen one cliff, you've seen them all. Myrtle Beach is much better."

Sylvia was aghast, "Myrtle Beach? Are you serious?"

Dink said, "Ed, trust me, the food there is terrible, the sunsets are rubbish, it rains all the time anyway. There are no nice bars and no good music—just a bunch of drunks strumming a song nobody ever heard of. There is no history whatsoever, and all those peat fires will make you sick to your stomach. Trust me, Ed. Myrtle Beach is much better."

For the next twenty minutes, Dink and Sylvia argued about Ireland. Edward sneaked inside the kitchen and poured himself a glass of sweet, muscadine wine while he waited for a truce or at least a break in the action. Finally, the steaks were done, the salads were eaten and the key lime pie was enjoyed. But the question of Ireland was never settled to the satisfaction of either Dink or Sylvia.

26

EDWARD WAS MAKING HIS WEEKLY VISIT to the YMCA, well almost weekly, and he had on a tee shirt from the University of North Carolina—Pembroke. He had bought it at a church yard sale. It was almost new and had a nice picture of an Indian brave on the front—Edward liked it. He was on his second set of arm curls, with twenty-pound weights, when an older gentleman walked up to him and asked had he attended UNC-Pembroke. "No," Edward answered, "I just liked the shirt, it's nice. In fact, I've never been to Pembroke; don't even know where it is."

The older man seemed a bit disappointed, and said, "My daughter went there to get her teaching degree and her Master's."

Edward said, "I'm sure you're proud of her, sir. My name's Edward, but some people call me Ed."

"I'm Dr. Bender, Edward. Nice to meet you."

"Are you at the hospital or in practice for yourself, Dr. Bender?"

"I have a practice over off Hawthorne Road, I specialize in gastrointestinal disorders."

Edward perked up, "I have a friend who goes to your office, Mr. Cleveland—you probably don't know him."

"Oh, I know Mr. Cleveland alright. Everybody knows Mr. Cleveland."

Edward smiled and said, "Yeah, I know what you mean, but still, it's sad what's happening to him."

Dr. Bender replied, "Sad? What's sad? That Dink thinks he knows everything in the world about medicine?"

"No, it's sad that he's dying. He just seems so full of life."

"Dying?" Dr. Bender gasped, "Who's dying? Certainly not Dink Cleveland. He's too ornery to die, and he's in better health than anybody his age—even with the paralysis."

"He told me he had cancer and was dying, Doctor. Are you sure we're talking about the same man?"

"Paralyzed on one side, thinks he knows everything about everything, and always telling you useless trivial information? That's the Dink Cleveland I'm talking about."

Edward was flabbergasted. "You mean he's not dying?"

The doctor folded his arms and said, "Well, I guess we're all dying to some extent, Charles. But our Mr. Cleveland isn't in any dire straits—not by a long shot."

Edward was wondering who Charles was, and wondering why Dink kept telling him that he's dying. Then Dr. Bender said, "I'm sorry, your name's not Charles is it? I seem to have forgotten . . . I apologize."

"It's Edward. No problem, and thanks for setting me straight." Edward then watched Dr. Bender go the elliptical machine and take his tablet out to read something while he exercised. "So Dink is not dying?" Edward pondered this question for several moments until an elderly lady came up in front of him and asked how much longer he'd be on that machine. Edward said, "I'm leaving now, it's all yours, ma'am." He started to walk away and she yelled at him,

"Aren't you going to wipe it down?"

"Yes, ma'am . . . sorry." Edward cleaned the machine under the watchful gaze of this less than sociable old woman. He couldn't wait to call Sylvia and tell her the news he'd just gotten about Dink. As soon as Edward got home he started to take a shower but realized he hadn't actually sweated during his workout, so instead, he got a glass of sweet tea and sat down to call Sylvia. "Sylvia, you'll never guess what I found out today?"

Sylvia paused a moment then said, "That 60,000 plastic bags are being used in the U.S. every 5 seconds?"

"What? No, not that."

"That every day in the U.S. more than 100,000 people get a speeding ticket?"

Silence on Edward's end as he's trying to understand why she's telling him these senseless facts.

"That in 1824, Andrew Jackson won the popular vote and got the most votes in the Electoral College, but lost the presidential election anyway?"

"No. What? Really? How could that happen?"

"Edward, you are so innocent and naïve. You really need someone to take care of you and protect you."

Edward was so flummoxed that he didn't know what to say, so he just blurted out, "Dink is not dying. His health is fine."

After four or five seconds of silence, Sylvia said, "The oldest man in the U.S. just recently died. He was 111 years old. When interviewed, he put his long life down to a simple combination of good genetics, decent nutrition, exercise, and not having any children. Does Mr. Cleveland have any children?"

"No, he never married."

"The oldest woman in Japan said her secret to living a long life is to eat a good meal and relax. But there's a man in Denmark who is 115 years old and says his secret is: 'Friends, a good cigar, drinking lots of good water, no alcohol, staying positive, and lots of singing.' But Britain's oldest man puts his longevity down to 'cigarettes, whiskey, and wild, wild women.' Another 107-year-old man gave his secret as eating porridge, prunes, and never going to bed on a full stomach."

Edward held the phone to his ear and shook his head slowly, thinking, "Why did I call her?"

But she wasn't finished, "And NBC did an interview with a 100-year old doctor who still ran his own practice. He said, 'Exercise, to me, is totally unnecessary. I think it's overrated. The use of vitamins? Forget it. And I don't encourage going to a lot of doctors either. Fall in love, get married. Sex is to be encouraged. Choose the right parents. Have a pet. Life gets lonely sometimes. Pets are reminders of how we're all living things. And finally, try not to eat anything that's healthy. It's true! I eat whatever I want. The secret to longevity is ice cream.' Maybe you could share these thoughts with Mr. Cleveland, Edward."

Edward started thinking, "I wonder what she's wearing? She could have just stepped out of the shower and have nothing on . . . it's possible."

"Edward, are you there?"

Edward was shaken back to reality, but he quickly gave himself an out by saying, "Yes, those are great ideas. Thanks, honey. I'll call you later. Bye." Now, the overriding question was should he confront Dink with the news that he wasn't dying, or not. Hmm.

27

DINK ANSWERED THE PHONE CALL from Edward, who said, "Hey, Dink, I was thinking about coming over for a visit. Are you busy?"

"No, Ed, why would you think an old, worthless, crippled man like me would be busy?"

Edward thought to himself, "Is there any way to answer that without getting in trouble?" So he didn't. When the silence became overwhelming, Dink added, "Do you understand what karma is, Ed?" Before Edward could answer that, Dink continued, "It's knowing that Babe Ruth and Elvis both died on the same day of the year that Madonna was born. That's exactly what this world deserves, Ed. That, my friend, is karma." Before Edward could respond, Dink disconnected the phone call.

Edward arrived to find Dink sitting out by the lake, on the same bench, left of the middle. However, this time Dink was holding a glass of wine. Edward knew the residents were not supposed to bring any drinks, especially wine, out to the lake area. But, Dink was not just any resident. Edward sat at the end of the bench and waited for Dink to speak first. Dink didn't. They sat there for at least fifteen minutes in utter and complete silence. Then Dink rose, grabbed his cane and started shuffling back into the building. Edward didn't know what to do, so he let Dink get several steps ahead of him, then began following him inside.

Just before he got to the doorway Dink bent over and picked something up from the sidewalk. He looked at it closely then dropped it back on the walkway and went inside. Edward took a few steps and saw that it was a quarter that Dink had picked up and dropped back down. He didn't understand, but if Dink didn't want the quarter, neither did he. So he also dropped it back down on the sidewalk where he found it.

Dink ordered two glasses of red wine from the waiter. He took one and left the other for Edward. It was going to be that kind of day. After he took a good, sizeable swig from his wine, Dink said, "Ed, I want to tell you about someone . . . have you ever heard of Frank Sinatra?"

"Yeah, Dink, everybody's heard of Frank Sinatra."

"Did you know that when he was born the doctors thought he was dead? They laid him off to the side and attended his mother. His grandmother picked up the lifeless body and stuck him under some cold water, then old Frank belted out his first song, completely shocking the doctors. Maybe because of his birth, who knows, but he never grew like other kids did. He was only 5'7" and wore elevator shoes to make him seem taller.

In the 1940's when his publicist was trying to garner attention for Frank, he would audition girls for how loud they could scream. Then he paid them five bucks and placed them strategically in the audience to whip up excitement. In the 1950's his success began to waiver because the girls all liked a new singer, Eddie Fisher. Frank became despondent, and one day went back to his home, put his head in the stove and turned on the gas. Luckily for him, his manager found him in time and saved him. He made three other suicide attempts, all of them in the throes of his volatile relationship with Ava Gardner.

His drink of choice was a mix of four ice cubes, two fingers of Jack Daniel's whiskey, and a splash of water. He once said, 'This is a gentleman's drink.' Remember Mia Farrow, Ed? He married her in 1966, but only for two years—he was too old for her. Frank had his lawyer serve her the divorce papers while she was on the set of the film 'Rosemary's Baby.' But, to show you how Frank was, jump ahead to the 1990's when Mia Farrow was publicly humiliated by her long-term lover's, Woody Allen, marriage to their adopted daughter. Sinatra offered to have Allen's legs broken. An obvious connection to Sinatra's Mafia relationships. Mia declined.

Later in life, when his only son, Frank, Jr., was kidnapped, the kidnappers demanded that he call from an untraceable pay phone. This event led him to a life-long habit of carrying a roll of dimes in his pocket. The kidnappers demanded $240,000 for the safe return of his son. He had to use the pay phones to talk to the kidnappers and always needed dimes to pay the phone charges. After Frank, Jr. was released unharmed, Sinatra always carried a roll of dimes in his pocket—he was even buried with a roll of dimes in his pocket.

What most people don't know was that he also starred in 58 films and won an Academy Award for one of them. He and Sammy Davis, Jr., Dean Martin, Peter Lawford, and Joey Bishop made up the infamous 'Rat Pack.' They did films together and played in Las Vegas with each other. He married four times, the last time to the former wife of Zeppo Marx. There will never again be anyone like old Frank, Ed. He was one-of-a-kind."

When he finished his story of Frank Sinatra, Dink looked over at Edward, who asked, "You're not really dying are you, Dink?"

"Of course I'm dying, Ed. So are you and everyone else on this planet. Do you think you're going to get out alive?"

"But you lead me to believe you're close to dying now."

"I might be, Ed. We can't predict how long we have. I might die tonight, or I might die ten years from now. But trust me, son . . . we're all dying, we just don't know when."

Edward leaned forward and said, "But right now, you're fine . . . is that right?"

"Ed, look at me! I'm old, I'm crippled, I'm paralyzed, I'm mean and nasty, and fed up with people. Does that sound like I'm fine?"

Edward decided to let it go. There was no way he was going to win this discussion. As Dink started on his second glass of wine, Edward asked him, "Why did you tell me that story of Frank Sinatra? Was he one of your heroes?"

"Hero? Sinatra? I don't think so. I was only trying to enlighten your horizons, Ed. Would you rather hear about someone you don't know?" Before Edward could answer, Dink continued, "Let me tell you about a man named Paul Dirac. Do you know him, Ed?"

"Nope."

"He discovered things about quantum mechanics that men never knew existed. When asked to explain his theories, he said, 'They cannot be explained in words.' He had an unhappy childhood, but never mentioned it. So he learned to speak French, German, and Russian. He gets interested in mathematics and ends up at Cambridge, where he's famous for his long silences.

He made discoveries in quantum mechanics that involve no experiment, no apparatus, and no observation. He relaxed by climbing trees in a three-piece suit. He won the Nobel Prize and published a textbook, yet remained basically silent. He finally married, moved to America and lived a quiet life. He addressed mysteries and solved them mysteriously. His discoveries were like exquisitely carved statues falling out of the sky, one after another. He seemed to be able to conjure up laws of nature from pure thought. His imagination was on the scale of Einstein, Newton, and Darwin, but he was so simple that when his wife asked him, 'What would you do if I left you?' He thought for a while, then answered, 'I'd say, Goodbye, dear.'

Did you like that story better, Ed?"

"Well . . ."

28

TUESDAY NIGHT WAS EDWARD AND SYLVIA'S TELEVISION NIGHT together. They would have a light meal, pop some popcorn and try to find a movie they both enjoyed and play the game of, "How far will Sylvia let Edward go tonight?" They had BLT's for dinner and Sylvia was getting the popcorn out of the box when the phone rang. She called out to Edward and asked him to answer it for her, which he did. "Hello."

"Ed? Is that you?"

"Dink? Why are you calling Sylvia?

"Because she asked me to, not that it's any of your business."

Edward put his hand over the phone speaker and called out to Sylvia, "It's Dink. Did you ask him to call you?"

"Yes. Thanks, I'll be right out."

She came out, took the phone from Edward, sat down on the couch, and said, "Yes, Mr. Cleveland, I verified that. And that's not all, Louisiana has the Lake Pontchartrain Bridge that is the longest continuous bridge passing over water. It's nearly 24 miles long and for about 8 of those miles, you can't even see land. Uh, huh . . . uh huh . . . Well, Minnesota has more shoreline than the combined shorelines of California, Florida, and Hawaii—nearly 90,000 miles in total." A few moments of silence, then, "Well that's nothing . . . St. Louis hosted the 1904 Olympics, which was widely considered to be one of the weirdest games ever held. Only 12 countries attended and the games lasted over five months. The oddest event was the marathon. One runner was chased out of the marathon by a pack of dogs, while the winner hitched a ride on a car for most of the race. Then there was a competitor who actually stopped during the marathon to take a nap—and still managed to come in fourth place!"

Sylvia got up from the couch and started pacing, then she stopped and said into the phone, "Well that's nothing, Mr. Cleveland. There are more unemployed workers in the United States than there are people living in the entire nation of Greece." Silence, silence, then, "Yes, I'm sure! I wouldn't make up something like that. And also, the highest point in the entire state of Florida is only 345 feet above sea level."

More silence as Sylvia started pacing furiously around the living room, then, "I've got one better than that, Mr. Cleveland. San Francisco hardly has any cemeteries. Land is too valuable out there. With few exceptions, no one is allowed to be buried or even cremated within the city limits. Most people are buried in a nearby town called Colma, which is known for having more dead residents than live ones—around 4 million dead, with only about 1500 alive. Their town motto, which is on their website is: 'It's great to be alive in Colma.'"

More pacing, more pacing, then, "I already knew that, Mr. Cleveland. Yes, I did! I promise you I did." Silence, then, "I knew that as well. Oh yes, I did! Fine . . . goodbye!"

She set the phone down, looked over at Edward and asked, "Did you find us a good movie?"

Edward was stunned by what just happened. He said, "What was that about?"

"Sometimes Mr. Cleveland will call and ask me about things. That's all. There's nothing to it."

"Dink is calling you every week asking about things?"

"Well, more like every day."

"I can't believe this. Dink is talking to you more than I am."

At this point, Sylvia sat on the couch next to Edward, cuddled up close, and said, "Maybe we could skip the movie and popcorn tonight."

The next day Edward visited Dink with the intention of asking about the phone calls to Sylvia. He found Dink out by the lake, left of the middle, but the wind was blowing fairly hard. When he walked up to the bench, Dink said, "Let's go inside, this wind is bothering me."

When they sat down, Edward commented, "That's quite a windstorm out there today."

"Ed, you don't know what a windstorm really is. Back in 1934, a massive storm sent millions of tons of topsoil flying from across the parched Great Plains region of the United States as far east as New York, Boston, and Atlanta. Throughout history, these plains were covered in natural grasses which kept the soil from blowing away. But by the early 20th century farmers had plowed under much of the grass to create fields. This plowing continued for years and the invention of powerful gasoline tractors sped up the process.

That year, a severe drought spread across the region. As crops died, the wind began to carry dust from over-plowed and over-grazed lands. Over a two day period in 1934 high-level winds carried some 350 million tons of silt all the way from the northern Great Plains to the eastern seaboard. Even some ships that were 300 miles offshore saw dust collect on their decks.

These storms forced thousands of families to uproot and migrate to California, which caused the beginnings of what was known as the Great Depression. You're lucky you weren't alive back then, Ed. You'd probably be a California native, rather than a Tarheel. Do you like the Tarheels, Ed?"

"Nope," Edward thought, "ain't no way in the world I'm answering that." Instead, he asked Dink, "You want a glass of wine?"

Wine always made everything a little better. When he brought the wine back to Dink, he asked him about the call last night to Sylvia. "She told me something about Michael Jordan that I just didn't believe, Ed, and I had to check it out. She said that there have been 32 versions of the Jordan sneaker and the Jordan brand brings in more than $3 billion a year in worldwide sales. With Michael himself getting about $140 million each year in royalties. I didn't believe it was that much, but she was right. You'd better keep her, Ed. She can teach you some things."

Edward instantly remembered last night, and instead of popcorn and a movie, Sylvia did teach him some things.

"And you know what else she told me? She said there's a town right here in North Carolina that's called 'Whynot.'

It has its name because as the residents were arguing over a name for the town, someone stood up and said, 'Why not name the town Why Not and let's go home?' And so they did. Of course, I didn't believe that either, so I looked it up, and guess what, Ed. She was right again. But I got her back pretty soon. I told her there's a town called 'Big Ugly' in West Virginia. She didn't believe it, but she found out it was true."

Dink told Edward he had an appointment to get his toenails clipped and he needed to get moving. Edward walked with him down the long hallway to the manicurist's office. There was a sign on the door that read, "Be back in 10 minutes." Dink opened the door and went in any way. Edward stayed outside and waited. About 5 or 6 minutes later a young Asian lady came down the hallway and asked Edward if he had an appointment. He told her he had accompanied Mr. Cleveland, who was waiting inside. She rolled her eyes a bit and said, "His cereal never gets soggy. It sits there, staying crispy, just for him."

29

"ED, HAVE YOU EVER REALIZED HOW LUCKY the United States was on 9/11?"

Edward, who had just walked in the door, hadn't even realized Dink was there. He didn't see him out at the lake, so he walked in the doorway and was met by that question. "I didn't think we were lucky at all, Dink. In fact, we were pretty unlucky, wouldn't you agree?"

"No, Ed, I wouldn't agree. Those terrorists could have killed many thousands more if we hadn't been lucky. Do you realize that on any given day, over 50,000 people worked in the World Trade Center? Just think what the casualties could have been?"

Edward did not want to think about that . . . no one did.

"During the cleanup, along with 1.4 million tons of debris, they also removed 19,435 body parts. Think about that, Ed." Edward didn't want to think about that either.

"A month before 9/11, President Bush was handed a memo titled: 'Bin Laden Determined To Strike in US' saying it would be by hijacking planes, possibly targeting New York City. Did you know that, Ed?"

Edward was beyond the point of responding any longer.

Dink continued his somber monologue, "The 9/11 attacks also destroyed $100 million in art, including work from Pablo Picasso. On that fateful day, four people in the South Tower managed to escape from a floor above the plane's impact. For those who jumped from the towers, the fall lasted 10 seconds. They struck the ground at just under 150 miles per hour, enough to ensure instant death on impact. The last survivor was removed from the debris of the North Tower 27 hours after its collapse. The New York

Times wrote an article about every single 9/11 victim . . . they didn't have to do that, Ed . . . but they did."

Dink had not touched his glass of wine. He continued, "The man who ordered the grounding of all aircraft in the U.S. on 9/11 was on his first day on the job. There was only one plane allowed to take off after flights were grounded. It was a plane carrying antivenin to a man bitten by a highly venomous snake. The largest sea evacuation in the U.S. happened on 9/11. Almost 500,000 people got evacuated by boat in less than 9 hours."

Dink then took a small sip of wine and said, "One month before 9/11, the actor James Woods reported 4 suspicious individuals on his flight. Authorities did not act on his claim and they later turned out to be the 9/11 hijackers. And, Ed, one final sad, sad story from that terrible day . . . the World Trade Center's most famous survivor and president of its support group, a lady named Tania Head, was later found to be a fraud. She wasn't even in New York on 9/11."

Edward was silent. What could he say? Dink picked his wine glass up, then sat it back down. He then picked up his cane and shuffled off to his room.

<hr>

Edward called Sylvia and asked if he could come over. He told her his meeting with Dink had left him feeling a little depressed. Sylvia volunteered to order a pizza for them, she knew pizza would always cheer up Edward. She also had a glass of sweet tea waiting for him when he arrived and wore a top that she knew would cheer him up. She was right.

Edward's mood was immediately elated upon seeing Sylvia. She handed him the sweat tea and gave him a rather lengthy kiss, which improved his mental state even further. Edward was rather excited and hoping for even more than pizza and sweet tea when Sylvia pulled him to the couch. But as soon as she sat down, she looked at Edward and said, "Have you ever wondered why deer keep jumping in front of cars, honey?"

Edward was certain he'd misunderstood her, so he said, "What?"

"Deer, Edward, they have great vision, but why do they keep jumping in front of cars and killing themselves? Have you ever wondered about that?"

"Umm . . . no."

"Well, I have. I looked it up—deer are hit by cars about 1.5 million times a year. A million and a half, Edward! And you know why I think that happens?" Before Edward could answer, she continued, "Because God created them with a lesser instinct so they aren't as smart as us humans. Plus, if deer weren't killed, crows and turkey vultures would have nothing to eat. So have no fear, honey, if you run into a deer, it may ruin your car, but you also helped feed many other animals their dinner."

Edward took a small sip of his tea, glanced forlornly at Sylvia's alluring top, yet knew, this wasn't the end of the story. It wasn't. "Deer are not used to fast objects coming directly at them, Edward. It's not in their evolution to know what a car is. Same reason why you see squashed squirrels, rabbits, skunks, and possums. Nothing in their world moves faster than they do. So they are completely confused and unable to cope with cars that are relatively quiet and move so quickly. The headlights at night make it even more difficult for them to know what to do.

Plus, deer rarely look up, which is why smart deer hunters perch in tree stands. By the time they rush into traffic, they become spooked because they think they hear a predator—then, it's too late. But, Edward, the main reason for all these collisions is that deer don't practice safe sex. They are more focused on reproducing than safety. Most collisions occur in November when males are in rut, or heat, and are just oblivious about anything else—sort of like you are sometimes, Edward."

Edward didn't deny that. "And a lot of good grazing grasses grow along the shoulders of the roads too, which attracts them even more. All this contributes to the problem, honey. It's sad isn't it?" Edward didn't answer because he was still thinking about rutting and being in heat—similar to the way he was feeling right now. Just as Edward was going to act on his natural instincts, the doorbell rang. Pizza had arrived! For maybe the only time in his life, Edward was disappointed with pizza.

30

"ED, DID YOU KNOW THAT THE PLANET VENUS revolves opposite of what the earth and other planets revolve? Why does it do that? Do you know?"

Edward only wanted a glass of sweet wine on his daily visit. He didn't want to be quizzed on cosmic matters. "No, Dink. I have no clue."

"No one does, Ed. That's what's so strange. None of these so-called scientists have any idea in the world why it does that. And that's not all, Ed. Venus revolves on its own axis so slow that its days are longer than its years. Can you believe that?"

Edward was sipping a glass of Carlos grape wine that he hadn't tasted before. It was sweet and aromatic, Edward thought it might be the best glass of wine he'd ever had. He wasn't paying any attention at all to Dink. Dink, of course, knew that, but he didn't stop, "Ed, an NFL team does more laundry in one week than an average American family will do in two years." He looked over at Edward who was staring at his nearly empty glass and savoring the lasting joy of his newfound best friend.

"And did you know that spiders can survive for hours underwater by putting themselves in a self-induced coma?" Dink was wasting his time. Edward was already thinking of his next glass of Carlos. So, for the ONLY time in their relationship, Dink made something up simply to test Edward and see if he was listening, "Ed, it has been proven that men who have wild sexual encounters, including several kinds of depraved and forbidden sexual acts, tend to have an overwhelming desire for sweet wines. Did you know that?" Edward decided to refill his glass. He stood up, looked down at Dink and said, "That's very interesting

Dink. I didn't know that." However, the only thing he was really thinking was, 'I hope they haven't run out of this wine.'

When he returned to his seat, Dink began again, "Have you ever heard of a man named Dick Fellows, Ed?"

Edward's attention was focused now that his wine glass was full, "No, Dink, I don't think I have. Who is he?"

"Not who IS he, Ed, but who WAS he? Long ago, in the old west, he was an inept horseman who spent five years in San Quentin prison. Like many western bandits, Fellows drifted into a life of crime when his efforts to make an honest living failed to provide a decent income. He had planned on becoming a lawyer, but the outbreak of the Civil War put his ambitions on hold. He was fighting for the Confederacy when he was captured in 1863, while still in his teens. He spent the rest of the war in a northern prison camp. After the war, he returned home to Kentucky and tried to obtain his license to practice law, but drinking apparently interfered with his plans."

Edward seemed interested in the story and was slowing sipping his wine, trying his best to stay focused. "Soon, he headed west and traveled all the way to California in 1867, but he failed to prosper there either. Low on funds, he began robbing stagecoaches near Los Angeles, which was only a dusty, little town in those days. He adopted the name Dick Fellows to hopefully conceal his identity. He found that robbing stages provided a reasonably good income. When he sensed the local lawmen were closing in on him, he fled the area. In an effort to go straight, he and a partner bought 600 hogs, but soon thereafter a fire burned the operation to the ground and killed most of the hogs."

Edward was getting a little antsy as his glass of wine was nearing the bottom, but the story now had him attracted. "Soon, Fellows started robbing stages again. He concocted a plan to hold up a coach carrying Wells Fargo's chief detective at the time. Fellows reasoned that if the coach was carrying such an important man, it must be carrying a lot of money. He was right. The coach was carrying $240,000—a fortune in those days. However, he missed his chance to rob the stage when the horse he had stolen threw him, knocking him cold for several hours. He refused to walk away with nothing, so he stole a second horse and held up a different stage. He got a large strong box but realized the tools he needed to open the strong box were on his first stolen horse. When he tried to lift the box on to his horse's saddle, he startled his mount, and it, too, raced off, leaving him alone in the desert with night approaching.

At this point, Edward held up a finger at Dink, at said, "Just a minute." He ran over to the wine table, refilled his glass, and hurried back. "Okay, go ahead, Dink."

Dink understood. "Fellows had little choice but to lug the heavy box by hand. In the darkness, he fell over a high bluff, knocking himself unconscious for the second time that day. When he came to, he discovered that his left leg was broken and the treasure box had crushed his left foot. He managed to limp to a nearby construction camp, where he fashioned a crude pair of crutches and used a stolen ax to break open the box. The $1800 he found inside was trivial to the $240,000 he had missed, but it was better than nothing."

Edward was happy with the wine and thrilled with the story. "Unfortunately for Fellows, the Wells Fargo detectives soon tracked him down before he could spend his ill-gotten money. He was sentenced to eight years in San Quentin prison. He was a model prisoner and was pardoned in 1881. He made another attempt at honest living, but the money he was making, working for a newspaper and teaching Spanish, wasn't enough to satisfy the lifestyle he had become accustomed to. So, he started robbing stages again and by the time he was recaptured in 1882, he had become a celebrity. This time he went to jail in San Jose, where he received more than 700 visitors.

He eventually ended up at Folsom Prison where he devoted some of his time teaching a course in moral philosophy to his fellow inmates. He was pardoned at the age of 62, which is when he returned to his home in Kentucky and faded from the historical record. Except for his inept horsemanship and astonishingly bad luck, one biographer noted, 'For daring alone, he is the equal of any outlaws with whom I ever had dealings.'"

Edward was transfixed by the story, although, he may have been just a little tipsy—for the first time in his life. He sat there with his mouth half-open looking at Dink, waiting on something . . . anything. Finally, Dink helped him and said, "Your glass is empty."

Edward made it home, although he lied to Dink about his apparent sobriety level. However, he only made it as far as the lazy boy in the den. He leaned back in the chair and propped his legs up and fell fast asleep. He didn't wake until the phone disturbed him a few hours later. It was Sylvia wondering where he was. He barely knew where he was and had no idea what time it had become. He was not good at lying and even worse at concealing anything from Sylvia. "What happened to you? Where have you been? Was something else more important than seeing me? Did you forget about me, Edward?" Edward had no answer to any of these questions, so he quite cleverly said nothing. "Edward? Are you there?"

"Yes, honey, I was stopping to get you a present, I'll be there shortly." Ooh . . . this made things better.

"Okay, I was a little worried, you're never late. But I understand now, with the present and all. See you soon. Oh, and Edward, don't forget to pick up a bottle of Merlot for our dinner."

Edward nodded into the phone as he thought to himself, "Merlot?? You cannot be serious!" But, instead, he said, "Okay, honey." And wondered what sort of present he now had to buy.

31

"ED, WHY DON'T YOU BRING SYLVIA around anymore? She used to come with you quite frequently . . . what happened?"

Edward smiled very coyly and answered, "Maybe we have some things we like to do that require a little privacy, Dink."

"No . . . really, why doesn't she come anymore? Is it because I might intimidate her a little?"

"I don't know, Dink, I guess there are some things only God knows."

"I thought you didn't believe in God, Ed. You keep avoiding the subject every time I ask."

"I never said that, Dink. Just because I don't want to get into an argument with you is no indication of my beliefs in God, or anything else, for that matter. In fact, I have a pretty solid foundation of beliefs in God, not that it's any of your business."

"Really? Tell me about it."

Edward thought to himself, "Dang, now I've done it." So he quickly thought that if he brought up his mother, maybe Dink wouldn't be so hard on him. "My mother taught me all about God, Dink. I remember one of the most important things she taught us all from the Bible was that 'God helps those who help themselves.' That always instilled a good work ethic in us." Edward was proud of that answer. There was no way Dink could contradict the Bible AND his mother.

At first, Dink didn't say anything, then he nodded a little before he spoke . . . but he did speak. "Ed, I want to tell you a little story: One time there was a flood in this town and this one man sat out on his steps watching the flood waters rise around his home. After an hour or two, a small boat came by and some men on the boat said, 'We're here to rescue you. Hop in.' The man looked at them and replied, 'No thanks, God'll save me.'

The flood waters continued to rise and the next day the man had to climb up in his balcony to stay out of the water. Another boat came by and stopped, the men yelled at him again, 'Hop in the boat, sir, we're here to rescue you.' Again, the man said, 'No thanks, God'll save me.' Overnight the waters kept rising and by the next day, the man was clinging to his chimney to stay out of the raging waters. Finally, a helicopter came and hovered over the man, dropping a basket for him to climb into. From a loudspeaker, one of the men in the helicopter said, 'Climb in, sir, we're here to save you.' Once again the man replied, 'No thanks, God'll save me.'

Well, Ed, the man drowned in that flood. When he got to heaven and St. Peter met him at the gates, the man was still pretty upset that God hadn't saved him—and told Peter so. Peter shook his head back and forth, then said, 'Sir, He sent two boats and a helicopter and you refused them all.'

Ed, that man is me and you and everyone else alive in the world today. And let me tell you something else, and I apologize to your mother because I'm sure she had good intentions with all her lessons for you. Nowhere in the Bible does it say, 'God helps those who help themselves.' That line came from some fairy tales and stories people wrote and most famously came from something Benjamin Franklin wrote—not from the Bible. In fact, Ed, the Bible teaches the exact opposite of that line, doesn't it? That God helps those who CAN'T help themselves. Right?"

"No, that can't be right." Edward thought. But there was no way he was going to contradict Dink . . . not about this, or anything else, really. Dink was always right. Edward thought about asking him, "Are you sure?" But he knew the answer to that as well. He wished he had a glass of wine, or two.

Later that night, after he and Sylvia had finished their BLT's and sweet tea, Edward asked her the question that had been gnawing at him all day, "Honey, doesn't the Bible say, 'God helps those who help themselves?'"

"Of course it does, Edward. Everybody knows that."

"Well, Dink said that line is not in the Bible. That the Bible, in fact, teaches the exact opposite of that line." Sylvia rose immediately from the table, walked over to a small desk, grabbed her Bible, and went to her computer. Edward saw all this, knew what she was going to do, and thought to himself,

"Idiot! Keep your mouth shut."

She started flipping pages and banging on that keyboard so fast that Edward thought they both might catch on fire. Eventually, after being ignored for an insufferable period of time, he quietly excused himself and went home. When he walked out the door, she was still flipping pages and banging away, in absolute obliviousness to him leaving. He shut the door and started walking to his car, and once again thought to himself, "Idiot!"

Edward started to have a glass of peach wine before he went to bed but decided against it. He just brushed his teeth, picked up a Sandra Brown novel and laid down. Before he got to the second page, his phone rang . . . Sylvia. He started not to answer, just to teach her a lesson—but thought better of it. "Hello."

"Edward, I'm not giving up, but I haven't found that sentence in the Bible yet. However, I did find something else very interesting . . . Charles Lindbergh was not the first man to fly across the Atlantic Ocean. He wasn't even the second, third, or 50th! Lindbergh was the 85th man to make the trip. However, he was the first to make it solo—that's what made him famous. And talking about flying, Edward, during WWII, the U.S. Army Air Forces lost 14,903 pilots and crew. Have you ever heard that before? In fact, during the war, more men died in the U.S. Air Corps than with the U.S. Marine Corps. For the Air Corps, the odds of being killed were 71 percent!

Also, Edward, Alexander Graham Bell wasn't the first person to invent the telephone. He was, however, the first one to patent it. An Italian guy first invented it but wasn't given credit for it until a hundred years after the fact—unbelievable. And guess what else I found out Edward . . ."

Edward had no clue what she found out, but he was wishing he'd poured himself a glass a peach wine—a big one.

"Napoleon Bonaparte wasn't really short. He was nearly 5 feet 7 inches tall, which was an average height for his time. Paintings depicted him short, so that's what people assumed. And guess what else people have been taught that's wrong, Edward." She didn't give Edward a chance to answer before she continued, "King Henry VIII of England didn't marry eight women at all. In reality, he married six women. And contrary to popular belief, he didn't kill all of them either. He divorced two of them, beheaded two others, another one died due to birth complications, and the final one survived him. Isn't that fascinating, Edward?"

Edward was not wondering about Henry VIII, nor about Alexander Graham Bell, nor even Charles Lindbergh . . . but he was wondering if it was too late for him to have a glass of peach wine. And, had Sylvia changed into her nightgown yet. Yes . . . that's what he was wondering about.

32

EDWARD AND SYLVIA ARRIVED at Arbor Acres to find Dink sitting in the lounge area with a plate of cheese squares and a healthy glass of red wine. Edward shook Dink's good hand, while Sylvia pecked him on the cheek, which made Dink almost smile. When they sat, Sylvia said, "Mr. Cleveland, I was quite surprised to learn that the sentence you told Edward about is, indeed, not in the Bible."

This news did make Dink smile, but he didn't gloat or say anything. So Sylvia continued, "But I did find something you might find very interesting." The smile quickly faded from Dink's face, as she said, "Winston Churchill, as a youth, once suffered a concussion and ruptured a kidney while playfully throwing himself off a bridge. Later on, he nearly drowned in a Swiss lake. He also fell several times from horses, and once he dislocated his shoulder while disembarking from a ship in India. He crashed a plane while learning to fly, and was hit by a car when he looked the wrong way trying to cross New York's Fifth Avenue. None of these incidents, however, left him too worse for wear. He lived until the age of 90 before finally succumbing to a stroke on the exact same day his father died, 70 years earlier. Pretty interesting isn't it? I bet you didn't know all that about Mr. Churchill, did you?"

Dink let that question settle for a moment, then succinctly answered, "Yes . . . I did."

It was as if someone had just stolen Sylvia's little puppy. She looked at Edward, then said, "In 1899, Churchill was held POW in Africa as a newspaper correspondent. After learning that his release was unlikely, he made a 300-mile escape by jumping from a freight train and walking." She looked at Dink while arching an eyebrow. Dink replied,

"It was South Africa, my dear . . . not Africa. Certainly, you should know the difference between the two." Sylvia could have spit fire—and almost did—as she continued,

"During his 1941 visit to the White House, Churchill spent much of his personal time naked and walking around his room drinking brandy. One day his towel fell off from around his waist in front of President Theodore Roosevelt, during a conversation. Without batting an eyelid, Churchill said: 'You see, Mr. President? I have nothing to hide.'" Sylvia was very proud of this story and the research it took her to find it. She looked at Edward, who was smiling, then at Dink, who answered,

"Sylvia . . . sweet, innocent, little girl. I'm sure you know, but seem to have forgotten, that it wasn't President Theodore Roosevelt at all, who witnessed that in 1941—but President Franklin Delano Roosevelt."

Sylvia was shocked and overwhelmed that she had inadvertently mixed the two presidents. She knew that! She knew more about FDR and Teddy than any crippled, old man did! She knew more than . . . well . . . anybody! Her mind was racing—what else? What else? Think, girl . . . then, "Once, during a visit to see the King of Saudi Arabia, Churchill was told he couldn't drink in front of the King, due to his religious beliefs. Churchill responded, 'My religion prescribes an absolute sacred rite of smoking cigars and drinking alcohol before, after, and if need be, during all meals and the intervals between them.'

The cigar shop owner where Churchill bought his cigars, estimated that he bought over 200,000 cigars from him in his lifetime. Although to be fair, he likely chewed his way through half of them. In fact, Churchill would usually slobber through a half-eaten Cuban cigar, before throwing it away. And, he loved to drink! He always had some alcohol in his system for most of his life, although he was very rarely drunk. The one famous instance he was drunk has been well-documented: At a party, a socialite woman walked up to him and scolded him saying, 'Sir, you are drunk!' He looked back at her and replied, 'Yes, I am. But tomorrow I'll be sober, whereas you, my dear, will still be ugly.'"

Sylvia was extremely proud of herself. She took Edward's hand and held it as she exulted over her story.

Edward then looked at Dink and asked, "How about that, Dink? Pretty good, huh?"

Dink was finishing eating a cheese square, and when he swallowed it, he took a small sip of wine and said, "Yes, fairly accurate, except that it wasn't a socialite he spoke to, it was a politician named Bessie Braddock."

After saying this, he popped another cheese square into his mouth. Sylvia stood up quickly and started walking towards the exit. Poor Edward didn't know what to do. When she got to the door, she turned around and looked back at Edward, who was still too stunned to move. So Dink said, "I think she wants you to follow her."

It was not a pleasant trip to Sylvia's house. They were supposed to go out and eat at Mama Zoe's restaurant, which they both loved. That got canceled. Sylvia, although not shedding tears, was very close to it . . . probably as close as she had ever been. She told Edward, "I just want to go home and humor myself—I feel terrible!"

Edward's mind raced. "No . . . concentrate," he thought. So, he kept quiet and walked Sylvia in the door. She told him to sit. He did. She went to her bedroom and soon came out with a magazine called "IQ" which Edward had never heard of. She sat down and said, "This always cheers me up, Edward. After that dreadful ordeal, I need something to make me feel better." Edward started to volunteer his services in the "cheering up" department, but he quickly realized the insanity of that thought. So he just sat there as Sylvia started reading.

She quickly flipped to the back of the magazine and said, "This is my favorite part—where these crazy celebrities show just how stupid they really are. Listen to some of these quotes, Edward. You won't believe it:

Brooke Shields

"Smoking kills. If you're killed, you've lost an important part of your life."

Deion Sanders

"When you say I committed adultery, are you stating it was before my marriage or prior to it?"

Jason Kidd – NBA player

"We are going to turn this team around 360 degrees."

Don King

"He speaks English, Spanish, and he's bilingual too."
Samuel Goldwyn
"I don't think anybody should write his autobiography until after he's dead."
Britney Spears
"I've never really wanted to go to Japan. Simply because I don't like eating fish. And I know that's very popular out there in Africa."
Christina Aguilera
"So, where's the Cannes Film Festival being held this year?"
Jessica Simpson
"Is this chicken or is this fish? I know it's tuna but it says chicken of the sea."
Arnold Schwarzenegger
"I think gay marriage is something that should be between a man and a woman."

Ginger Spice girl, Geri Halliwell
"First my mother was Spanish. Then she became a Jehovah's Witness."
Mike Tyson
"I guess I'm going to fade into Bolivian."
Dennis Rodman
"Chemistry is a class you take in high school or college, where they teach you that 2 plus 2 equals 10 . . . or something."
Sylvia was starting to smile a little when she came to the last one,
Mariah Carey
I just want one day off when I can go swimming and eat ice cream and look at rainbows."
Sylvia then added, "Me too, honey, me too."

33

EDWARD THOUGHT HE SHOULD DEFEND Sylvia's honor . . ."Dink, why did you have to demean Sylvia like you did? That wasn't very nice."

Dink kept his control and tried to stay calm. "Ed, would you rather I just let her go on thinking her mistakes were factual? Do you want to perpetuate falsehoods and lies? Is that what you want, Ed? Would you rather I say nothing and let her embarrass herself in front of others, who might not be as understanding as I am? Is that what you want, Edward?"

Edward thought he was right in questioning Dink. He thought he made some good points. He thought goodness and righteousness were on his side. Then Dink spoke and everything changed. Edward didn't know how to answer without furthering his predicament . . . so he wisely chose to be silent.

"Well, Ed? Are you going to answer me?"

Silence.

"What's wrong, is she not doing the dirty with you?"

"Dink!"

"She's cut you off, huh?"

"Dink, sometimes you can be a jerk. You know that?"

"Of course I do, Ed. I might be a jerk, among other things, but I'm not stupid."

"Well why do want to drive people away, Dink. Why can't you just be friendly?"

"Ed, I know you don't believe in God, but let me explain something to you . . ." Edward tried to object, but Dink wouldn't let him, "God made us all exactly like He wanted to make us. He doesn't make mistakes, Ed, like me and you and yes, like Sylvia does. 'Oops' is not in His vocabulary. He made me and you exactly like He wanted us to be. I am what I am. Just as you are who you are. I can't change—not long term—neither can you—neither can Sylvia. As much as she'd like to be like me, she can't. And I can't be like you—all nice and good and drinking sweet wine—I can't do it, Ed! God made me who I am. Now, if my personality bothers you too much, you can leave anytime at all—just like all the others have. But somehow, Ed, I thought you were different. I guess I was wrong."

Edward felt like he should apologize. Apologize for what? He didn't know. But he was certain he should apologize for something. Then Dink said, "Ed, do you remember Simon & Garfunkel?"

What an odd question to be asking at this point in the conversation, but Edward answered it, "Yes, Dink. They were famous, everybody knows them."

"I don't want us to end up like them. They were very successful, sold a lot of records, and got inducted into the Rock & Roll Hall of Fame. But in the end, they hated each other, Ed. At the induction ceremony, Simon, speaking of his partner, Garfunkel, said, 'Arthur and I agree about almost nothing, but it's true, I have enriched his life quite a bit.' Now that was a cruel thing to say about your life-long friend wasn't it, Ed? I would never say that about you. Remember that, Ed. Now go get us a glass of wine."

Edward did go get them a glass of wine . . . red and dry and sour for Dink. Sweet, lovely, and smooth for himself. All the while wondering if Dink had just insulted him, or had just apologized to him . . . he could not decide.

"Edward, I need to see Mr. Cleveland again . . . as soon as you can arrange it."

Edward could hardly believe what he was hearing. He thought Sylvia would never want to visit Dink again. "Okay, honey, if you're sure. Are you sure?"

"Yes, Edward, I'm a grown woman, I'm sure of what I want. And I want to prove to him that I'm not some forgetful ditz that he witnessed last time. I'll be ready. You just arrange it. Okay?"

The last "Okay?" wasn't really a question—and Edward knew it. It was an order to set it up quickly—and Edward knew that as well.

———◦———

"Sylvia, so good to see you again. My, you do look lovely today. Have you done something different with your hair?" Dink was trying—he really was.

Sylvia was almost flattered, but she, too, knew Dink was really trying—not to tell the truth—but to make amends. "Thank you, Mr. Cleveland. I was wondering if you had the time to listen to some thoughts I have and to let me know if you think they're accurate?" That's not at all what Sylvia was thinking. She knew good and well all her facts were accurate. She double and triple checked everything—twice! She was hoping Dink would contradict something just so she could discipline him.

"Certainly, Sylvia. I'm honored that you would think enough of me to ask. Please, go ahead." Edward was on pins and needles. They were both being a little too nice and too polite . . . there was no way this was going to end peacefully and harmoniously. He knew it.

Dink had no idea what subject Sylvia would be starting with, but he was a tad surprised when she started talking about Vietnam.

"Mr. Cleveland, the United States never did declare war on Vietnam. Our government referred to it as a conflict. And contrary to common belief, nearly two-thirds of American men serving in the war were volunteers!" She looked over at Edward to make sure he was duly impressed with this fact. If the truth were to be known, Edward was more impressed with his vantage point of seeing Sylvia cross her legs in a rather short skirt.

"And, did you know this, Edward: During WWII, an average soldier saw about 40 days of combat in four years; while during the Vietnam War, there were, on average, 240 days of combat in one year! And, this so-called war lasted approximately 20 years, Edward, the longest war in the entire history of the United States."

She looked over at Dink for the first time. He noticed her glance and took that opportunity to reach across the table and grab a couple of grapes to pop into his mouth. She continued, "Vietnam veterans are often neglected and stereotyped, Edward. In fact, these veterans are less likely to be in prison—only one half of 1% of them have been jailed for crimes and they have a lower unemployment rate than the same non-vet groups." She stopped to let this fact sink in while she took a drink from her bottled water. Then she resumed,

"At the end of the war, the USS Midway crew pushed $10 million worth of helicopters into the sea so that a Cessna full of evacuees could land on the deck. During the actual war years, about 125,000 Americans fled to Canada to avoid the draft. About half of them returned when President Carter granted them amnesty on his first day in office. There were all sorts of men in that war, Edward. One man who won the Congressional Medal of Honor admitted he was high on marijuana when he single-handedly fought off two waves of Vietcong troops while he dragged a wounded soldier to safety. The shooter in the infamous Vietcong execution photo, that we've all seen a thousand times, opened a pizzeria in suburban Virginia after the war. He was only following orders and would have been shot himself if he hadn't done what he did."

Edward remembered that awful photo and his mind was temporarily displaced from Sylvia's legs to that frightful and gruesome image.

"That war made men do things they would never have thought of before: A U.S. task force known as 'Tiger Force' routinely cut off the ears of its victims to make necklaces from them. Navy Seal teams One and Two amassed a combined kill/death ratio of 200:1. The war also saw incredible acts of bravery, such as one Roy Benavidez, who performed possibly the most heroic six hours of battle any soldier ever has. When faced with over 1,000 Vietcong troops, he flew into a gunfight to save 12 Special Forces soldiers, with a knife as his only weapon. He was shot multiple times and believed dead until he spit in the face of the medic trying to put him in a body bag. It took 13 years to get him the Medal of Honor."

Dink and Edward thought about that. Neither man commented. What could they say?

"Superglue was used during the war to slow the bleeding until soldiers could get to a hospital. And duct tape was used to repair helicopter rotor blades. The United States alone suffered 58,220 deaths in the war. More than 3 million people died in total. The average age of Americans that died in that war was just over 23 years. 11,465 of them were under the age of 20."

All three of them stopped everything they were doing except breathing.

Finally, Sylvia regained enough composure to continue, "During that war, our national debt increased by $146 billion. And I learned that the founder of FedEx served two tours of duty in Vietnam and was awarded a Bronze Star, a Silver Star, and two Purple Hearts. And you know what I found fascinating about this entire sad ordeal, Edward? 91 percent of Vietnam veterans say they are glad they served. And, 74 percent said they would serve again, even without knowing what their fate would be. Would you do that, Edward?"

Edward was glad he didn't have to answer that question.

34

SYLVIA WAS PROUD OF HERSELF. Edward was proud of her. Dink was impressed and silently running over those facts in his mind so he wouldn't forget them. Sylvia asked him, "Did it all sound accurate to you, Mr. Cleveland?"

"Sylvia, you did a fantastic job. A lot of people have forgotten about our war heroes, especially those from Vietnam. I'm glad you haven't. Can I tell you a few similar facts from a different war? WWII."

"We'd love to hear them, Mr. Cleveland, wouldn't we Edward?"

This was another question Edward was glad he didn't have to truthfully answer.

"Sylvia, Hitler was an evil man, as we all know. His plan for Moscow was to kill all its residents and cover it with an artificial lake. However, more Germans were killed by the Russians in the Battle of Stalingrad alone than were killed or wounded by Americans during the entire war. That quickly ended Hitler's schemes in Russia. About 5,500 WWII bombs are still discovered in Germany every year and defused—an average of about 15 per day."

Now it was Dink's turn to look at Sylvia to see if she was paying attention. He didn't care about Edward.

"Before the war actually started, when Germany was acting up and intimidating everyone, the only country in the entire world to protest against the German annexation of Austria in 1938, was Mexico." He let that fact sink in a few seconds, then repeated it, "Mexico. And, what a lot of people don't know is that during WWII, the Japanese invaded Alaska, and more Americans were killed or wounded defending Alaska than at Pearl Harbor."

Sylvia started to say something but stopped when Edward touched her leg. Dink continued, "Every single spy Hitler thought he had in Britain during the war was, in fact, a double agent under British control. Another sad fact that is lost on a lot of us, Ed, is that more people died in Auschwitz than the British and American losses of WWII combined."

Dink took a few moments to compose himself, then said, "Here's a big difference between us and them, Ed: During the war, Japan bombed China with fleas infected with bubonic plague. And they slaughtered as many as 30 million Filipinos, Malays, Vietnamese, Cambodians, Indonesians, and Burmese. Whereas, during the war, the U.S. Air Force dropped more than 5 million leaflets warning Japanese civilians to evacuate cities that were going to be bombed. And with all that happened during the war, Ed, think about this fact: At the beginning of WWII, the U.S. Army was smaller than the army of Portugal."

Sylvia's mouth dropped open at this fact. Edward noticed and bumped her arm a little. "But we recovered quickly and, of course, you know all about D-Day, right?" They were each afraid to answer that question, so Dink continued, "German casualties on D-Day were around 1,000 men, while Allied casualties were at least 10,000. Theodore Roosevelt, Jr. was the only General involved in the initial assault on D-Day, after insisting to his superiors to be one of the first ones off the boats. He survived, then died of a heart attack one month later.

The actor who played 'Scotty' on Star Trek was shot 6 times on D-Day: 4 times in the leg, one in the chest, and one through his finger. And even though the German Air Force outnumbered us 30:1 on D-Day, they didn't shoot down a single allied plane in air-to-air combat. On the night of the D-Day invasion, only 15% of paratroopers landed in the right place. The Allies parachuted dummies all over Normandy on D-Day to distract the Nazi gunners from the real paratroopers."

Sylvia ignored Edward's hand and wanted more from Dink. Edward was aware of this and took the opportunity to move his hand to places he otherwise would never move it to, as Dink continued, "The last German WWII POW's weren't released from the Soviet Union until 1956. A secret radio belonging to a British POW during the war was kept so well hidden that, when he visited the camp 62 years later, it was still there.

Japanese war criminal Tojo Hideki attempted suicide after the surrender. He was saved and resuscitated by Allied forces, who then hanged him! Japanese Kamikaze pilots were allowed to return to their base if they couldn't find a suitable target. One pilot was shot after his ninth return." Edward chuckled a little upon hearing this, but Dink's stern stare-down ended it quickly. "During the entire war, 47 Soviets died for every 1 American, Ed. And something hardly anyone knows . . . Rolex replaced, for free, all watches seized by the Germans from shot-down allied pilots during the war." Sylvia's lower jaw had again dropped slightly open. Edward was afraid to make any movements at all, so he kept still.

"During the war, the U.S. Navy partnered with the Mafia to protect our country's ports. And during the war, deliveries made by carrier pigeons were 95% successful." Dink laughed a bit at this last fact, happy he could end his soliloquy on a less than dreadful note. He then turned to Edward, who quickly removed his hand from Sylvia's thigh, and said, "Did you learn anything, Ed?"

Edward knew better than to try and answer that, so he kept quiet. Then Sylvia turned to look at him and asked, "Well, did you, Ed?"

That night as Edward lay in bed thinking about what might have been, he had the grand idea that he should learn something like Vietnam, or WWII, to impress people with. But what could he learn that Sylvia and Dink didn't already know? That was the tough part . . . not learning some trivial information, but finding something neither of them would be familiar with. As much as he tried to concentrate on different subjects and stimulating ideas, his dreams kept reverting back to the feel of his hand on Sylvia's upper thigh earlier that evening. He eventually thought to himself, "It's not easy being me."

The next day at work he daydreamed all day long about subjects he could learn to impress Sylvia and Dink with. It was hard-- they knew everything. When he got home that evening, he fixed himself a peanut butter sandwich and had a Diet Pepsi as he sat in front of his computer. He searched and Googled for two hours—no luck. He just couldn't find anything that they didn't already know. It was frustrating.

He finally turned on the television, as a diversion, really. There was some inane game show on and one of the answers to a question was "Robert Zimmerman." Edward had never heard of Robert Zimmerman before so he turned his attention to the screen to see who it was. Turns out Robert Zimmerman was the birth name of Bob Dylan. Edward didn't know that, and he was going to bet that Sylvia and Dink didn't either. Back to the computer and Google Bob Dylan—find stuff that they don't know—that was his assignment!

Oh, boy . . . Edward was getting excited. He found stuff he'd never heard before: Robert Zimmerman was born in 1941 in Duluth, Minnesota. He changed his name in 1962 to Bob Dylan. Most people assumed the name alluded to the poet Dylan Thomas because young Zimmerman tried to make people think he was cerebral. However, those who knew the young man are certain he chose the new name because of his admiration for the Green Bay Packers football legend Bobby Dan Dillon.

Dylan went to the University of Minnesota and pledged a fraternity there, Sigma Alpha Mu. But before becoming a "frat boy," he flunked out of school. While he was enrolled, he was known for scamming his friends out of cigarettes and articles of clothing. He soon met the girl who was to become his long-time girlfriend, Suze Rotolo. When she introduced him to her mother, he lied to her and told the mother that he had a degenerative eye disease that would eventually lead him to go blind. She would never trust him again.

Early in his career, he was playing a gig in Kansas City and the Rolling Stones band member, Brian Jones, was there. Dylan insulted him so vehemently that Jones broke down in tears. He also had a famous encounter with another British band—The Beatles. He met them in New York and was a fan of theirs because he heard the lyrics to their No. 1 hit "I Want to Hold Your Hand," which had a lyric that read, "I can't hide." Dylan mistakenly heard it as, "I get high." He assumed it was a reference to The Beatles and drug use, so he went to their hotel and introduced them to marijuana. At the time, their drug of choice was scotch and Coke, but after Dylan's visit, they soon became full-fledged pot smokers.

He's never had a No. 1 single but was still inducted into the Rock & Roll Hall of Fame in 1988, where in his acceptance speech, he first gave thanks, inexplicably, to both Muhammad Ali and Little Richard. Then he started insulting the Beach Boys', Mike Love. Obviously, he was still enjoying the effects of an earlier marijuana cigarette.

When Elvis died in 1977, Dylan, who was going through a divorce at the time, didn't speak for a week. The next year, 1978, he took a three-month course at the Vineyard School of Discipleship as part of his conversion to born-again Christianity. He now has nine grandchildren and sports a bumper sticker on his car that reads, "World's Greatest Grandpa."

Ever since 1988, he's been on his "Never-Ending Tour, in which he plays at least 100 concerts per year.

Edward finished the article on Dylan, leaned back in his chair, and said, "Wow!" He thought he'd hit gold.

35

EDWARD PRACTICED HIS BOB DYLAN SPEECH for hours. He knew it was going to blow them both away. He was so excited that when he picked up Sylvia to take her over to Arbor Acres, he completely forgot to open the car door for her. He opened his door and slid inside, then looked out the passenger window to see her still standing there waiting for him. He scurried out and ran around the car, only to be met with an icy stare. "Sorry, honey. I have something on my mind that I'm excited about."

"Well, you can forget about that, Edward. We're going to Mr. Cleveland's like we promised. And the way I'm feeling right now, you can probably forget about it later as well."

Edward was certain that when he impressed Sylvia with his newfound knowledge, she would change her mind about things "later tonight." Dink was sitting in his apartment waiting on them. He was listening to some music on his CD player—music Edward had never heard before. After Sylvia sat down, he walked over to the desk where the CD player was and saw an empty CD holder with the name on the front that read, "Live at Fillmore East." There was no singing with the music—only instrumentals, so far. Odd, he thought. Dink turned it down a little, but he didn't turn it off. Odd again, for Dink.

Dink offered them something to drink, and Edward answered for them both, "I'd like to tell you both about some information I came upon before we have any refreshments. I'm assuming you both know who Bob Dylan is, well, I bet you don't know this . . ." He then proceeded to tell them all the information he had studied and memorized. He nailed it, not stumbling or forgetting even the smallest detail. Edward was extremely proud of himself. He first looked at

Sylvia for her approval, then he turned towards Dink who said,

"Edward, go get Sylvia a glass of wine while I tell her about a really impressive American. Sylvia, Neil Armstrong is someone you should know about, not some . . . Anyway, young Neil fell in love with flying at an early age and earned his pilot's license on his 16th birthday. After graduating college, he became a test pilot and could fly over 200 different types of aircraft. One plane he piloted could reach a top speed of 4,000 miles per hour!"

As Edward went to the refrigerator, Sylvia moved to the open seat nearer Dink's chair, while he continued, "During the Korean War, he flew 78 combat missions and was shot down once, but managed to escape. He won 20 Air Medals for his missions. And, he didn't need to smoke any marijuana cigarettes while he was doing all this. When he and Buzz Aldrin landed on the moon's surface on Sunday, July 20th, 1969 it was a defining moment for our country, and indeed, for the world. He and Aldrin were convinced that the chances of their successful landing were no better than 50/50.

President Nixon and his staff were well aware of the odds and the president had a disaster speech ready in the event of a tragedy. Armstrong said about the liftoff of the historic Apollo 11 flight, 'It felt like a train on a bad railroad track, shaking in every direction. And it was loud, really loud.'" Just then, Edward came into the room carrying two glasses of wine. Dink waited until he sat down and said, "Did you know, Ed, that in 1963, major league baseball pitcher, Gaylord Perry—from here in North Carolina—was quoted as saying, 'They'll put a man on the moon before I ever hit a home run.' On July 20, 1969, one hour after Neil Armstrong set foot on the moon, Gaylord hit his first, and only, home run of his career."

Sylvia grabbed her glass and took a long drink. Edward started to as well but remembered it was a Cabernet Franc, so he set the glass back down. Dink continued, "Almost all the still pictures from that day are of astronaut Buzz Aldrin because Neil ended up with the camera. They stayed on the moon's surface 6 hours and 38 minutes. When they returned to earth, scientists weren't sure about any 'moon diseases' they may have contracted, so they made them stay isolated in an Airstream trailer for 21 straight days."

When he finished, Dink looked at Edward and asked, "There was a third astronaut who stayed with the spaceship and didn't walk on the moon that day. Do you know his name, Ed?" Sylvia blurted out,

"Alan Bean."

Dink cocked his head a little and asked, "Are you sure?"

Sylvia bit her lip and said, "Pete Conrad?"

"No, they were both on Apollo 12 . . ."

Sylvia closed her eyes tightly and bit her lip even harder, then exclaimed, "Michael Collins!"

"Right! Very good, Sylvia."

She smiled and took another large drink of her wine. Edward tasted his, but didn't really drink any as he added, "I knew that."

No one said anything. Dink and Sylvia both knew Edward did not know that answer. Edward knew that they knew he didn't know. It was best all-around for everyone to remain quiet and sip their wine.

On their drive home, Sylvia was distracted, looking out the window at a full moon, thinking about Neil Armstrong. Edward thought she was giving him the cold shoulder because his speech about Bob Dylan had not been as "educational" as hearing about astronauts. He brooded all the way to Sylvia's house, and when he turned the motor off, he just sat there. He wanted Sylvia to know he was upset. She finally said, "Edward, are you going to open my door or do I need to do it myself?"

He huffed a little and she asked, "Okay, what's wrong?"

"I know ya'll think I'm as dumb as a sheep walking off a cliff, but I'm not. Just because I don't study trivia like you do doesn't mean I'm stupid."

She grabbed his hand and stroked it a little and added, "We don't think that at all, Edward. In fact, sheep have a bad reputation. Actually, they have similar IQ's to cattle and are nearly as smart as pigs. And, listen to this, sheep are known to self-medicate when they have some illnesses. They will eat specific plants when they're ill that can cure them. There was one sheep who became famous because he hid in a cave for six years so he wouldn't have to get sheared. By the time they found him and trimmed him, there was enough wool to make 20 men's suits." Edward liked the way she was rubbing his hand. She could tell he liked it, so she continued, "There was also a sheep in Australia one time who had 89 pounds of fleece when they gave it a haircut."

Edward said, "Really?"

"Yes, and after a baby sheep is born, it can stand immediately, within minutes, and join the herd. However, if sheep fall down and are on their backs, they cannot get up without help. Remember the old days in tennis when they used to make strings out of sheep gut?

Edward had never heard of that before, but he nodded "yes" anyway.

"To make one tennis racket, the small intestines from 11 sheep were needed. And, Edward, sheep have excellent peripheral vision. Their large rectangular pupils allow them to see almost 360 degrees. In fact, they can see behind themselves without turning their heads! So, you see, honey, they aren't dumb at all, and neither are you."

Edward smiled and quickly hopped out of the car to run around and open Sylvia's door. The quicker he got her out of the car and into the house, the quicker she just might show her appreciation for how smart he really was. Men love to dream.

36

THE NEXT MORNING, BEFORE SYLVIA GOT OUT OF BED, she was still thinking of the conversations from the previous night, not about . . . She was flustered because she didn't contribute to the evening's festivities—well, at least not at Dink's apartment. Her mind began racing, thinking of all the tidbits of information she could have told Dink if only Edward hadn't told that stupid story about Zimmerman, or Dylan, or, whatever his name was.

All sorts of odd trivia began popping into her mind: "The CIA reads up to 5 million tweets a day. Surgeons who grew up playing video games make 37% fewer errors. Most people can survive for up to 2 months without eating; but only 11 days without sleeping. The eternal flame at John F. Kennedy's gravesite in Arlington National Cemetery has only gone out twice since 1963." She yawned and burped, then thought of some other fascinating pieces of information.

"Cleopatra lived closer in time to the first Moon landing than to the building of the Great Pyramid. Lighters were invented before matches. The population of Ireland is still 2 million less than it was before the so-called potato famine, 160 years ago." And just before she got out of bed, she thought of this: "In 1923, a jockey won a race at Belmont Park in New York despite being dead! He suffered a heart attack mid-race, but his body stayed in the saddle until his horse crossed the finish line." She was so excited thinking of all this information to tell Dink that she enthusiastically screamed out, "I can't wait!"

Edward rolled over and replied, "I'm sorry honey, but you'll have to. I need to get to work."

———————◆———————

That afternoon when Edward dropped by Arbor Acres, he couldn't find Dink anywhere. He wasn't in his apartment, he wasn't in the lobby drinking wine and eating cheese squares, and he wasn't out by the lake on his bench, left of the middle. One of the staff members who recognized Edward told him that an Arbor Acres van had taken some residents on a visit to a museum today—that's probably where Mr. Cleveland was. Edward decided he'd leave a message for Dink and go home early. He was still a little tired from his late night exertions at Sylvia's house. He left a short note on Dink's door, "Dropped by to see you, I'll call you later. Admireingly yours, Edward."

Not long after Edward left, the van pulled up at Arbor Acres and the old people slowly exited the vehicle—all but Dink, who was still arguing with the driver, Conrad. "Connie, you've got your facts all mixed up! Wilt said he made love with 20,000 women—not 10,000. And let me tell you something else about him: He was the only big man to lead the NBA in assists. And no one remembers that Chamberlain averaged 50 points a game one season. Just think about that, Connie . . ."

Conrad interrupted Dink and said, "My name's Conrad—not Connie."

"If Wilt only scored 27 points in one game, Connie, which by today's standards would get LaBron James national headlines, Chamberlain would have had to score 73 the next game just to maintain his average! Think about that!"

"My name is Conrad, Mr. Cleveland!"

Dink stopped for a couple of seconds and stared at Conrad, then continued, "And I bet you don't remember his Lakers' team in 1973 that won 33 games in a row, do you? Nor that he played every minute of every game for 8 straight years, all except for 8 minutes in one game when he got ejected for a technical foul. He was an incredible athlete, Connie, people just have no idea. He also read voraciously, spoke several languages, and loved to discuss philosophy."

Conrad wanted to say something, something not nice, but he also didn't want to lose his job. So, he only said, "I need to be going, Mr. Cleveland."

"I understand, Connie. It's been great talking with you. If you ever need any more information, just give me a call." Dink then rose and started shuffling towards the bus exit when he saw a nickel on the floor under a seat. He tried to use his cane to get the nickel out, but couldn't quite reach it properly. Conrad saw him and knew his reputation so he quickly jumped up, went over to the seat and bent over to get the nickel. Dink said, "Thanks, Conrad, most people don't appreciate money like we do, do they?"

Conrad finally smiled and responded, "No, Mr. Cleveland, I guess they don't."

Dink stopped long enough to have a couple of cheese squares on his way to the apartment, but no wine, the trip had him feeling a little tired.

Edward was home, sipping a Diet Pepsi in his underwear when the phone rang. He saw it was from Dink and was hoping Dink didn't want him to come back over to Arbor Acres. He started not to answer it, but he did anyway, "Hello."

"You misspelled 'Admiringly,'" and Dink hung up.

Edward didn't come back to Arbor Acres until Saturday afternoon. He found Dink in his apartment watching a golf tournament on television. Edward had never seen Dink watching any sporting event before, or rarely even mentioning sports, so this surprised him. Dink seemed to be engrossed and didn't offer Edward anything to drink, instead, he just waved his hand towards the kitchen— Edward understood. After he sat back down, Edward said, "I didn't know you were a golf fan, Dink."

"I suppose there's a lot you don't know, Edward."

Edward thought to himself, "Why did he just call me Edward instead of Ed? This can't be good."

Dink asked, "What did you and Sylvia do last night, Ed?"

"Umm, we ate pizza and watched a movie."

"No . . . after that."

"After what?"

"What did you do after you ate pizza and watched a movie, son? And you'd better not tell me you went to sleep!"

Edward was squirming in his seat, but finally said, "Dink, you know I don't want to talk about that."

"Aw, relax," Dink said, "I need to educate you a little bit, anyway. I'm going to tell you why golf is better than sex, Ed. Pay attention."

"Oh, no . . ."Edward thought. "Why didn't I stay home?"

Dink began, "First, a below-par performance in golf is considered darned good." Edward wasn't sure if he was supposed to laugh at that or not.

"You can stop in the middle and have a cheeseburger and a couple of beers." Edward thought,

"Yeah, okay."

"In golf, it's easier to find the sweet spot. And, foursomes are encouraged! You can still make money at golf as a senior, and your partner doesn't hire a lawyer if you play with someone else." Edward finally understood that Dink was trying humor. He liked it.

"You don't have to cuddle with your partner when you're finished, either. And you know what's best of all, Ed?"

Edward couldn't wait . . .

"When your equipment gets old, you can replace it!" Dink wanted to laugh at that last statement, but it seemed as though he had forgotten how.

Finally, Edward could join Dink in a conversation—he knew a little about golf. He told Dink, "The great baseball player, Hank Aaron, once said, 'It took me seventeen years to get three thousand hits in baseball. It took me one afternoon on the golf course.'" Edward smiled, it seemed as though Dink tried to, so Edward continued, "Jack Benny once said, 'Give me golf clubs, fresh air, and a beautiful partner, and you can keep the clubs and the fresh air.'" Then he asked Dink, "You know why I like golf?"

"No, Edward . . . tell me."

"You can pee in the woods without getting arrested. And, you can flirt with the 19-year old beer girl and not get beat up or put in jail."

Although Dink still didn't smile, he did hold up his glass of tomato juice in a toast. Edward was more proud of that gesture than he was of the several X-rated words he elicited from Sylvia last Wednesday night.

37

"ED, HAVE YOU EVER HEARD OF GEORGE MIKAN?"

"Umm, I think so. Was he the mayor of Chicago back during the riots in the 60's?"

Dink looked at Edward like he would have looked at his pet poodle who just pooped on the carpet. "No, Ed. Lord have mercy, son."

"Well, I'm sorry, Dink. The name is familiar but I don't know him. So, tell me . . . who is he?"

"He was the first true gate attraction in professional basketball. Back before LeBron, Kobe, Michael, Kareem, Wilt, or even Bob Cousy. Mikan drew fans at a time when the league's success was far from assured. In college at DePaul University, he blocked so many shots that the NCAA passed a rule prohibiting 'goaltending.' When he went to the pros he was considered 'unguardable' by most teams. At 6'10" he was the most dominant player in the country.

He could sink hook shots with either hand and rebound better than anyone. He was so dominant that the NBA, to prevent him from commanding every game, changed the rules of the game. He was the reason they widened the free throw lane to 12 feet, from 6 feet, and why they instituted the 3-second rule. Even with the new rules, his team won the NBA championship in 1948, 1949, 1950, 1952, 1953, and 1954. He wasn't only the best player on the best team, he was the reason people went to the games—so they could say they saw the great George Mikan play.

When his team, the Minneapolis Lakers (who later moved to Los Angeles) played the New York Knicks at Madison Square Garden, the marquee outside read, 'George Mikan vs.

Knicks.' IN 1950, the Associated Press named Mikan the best basketball player of the first half of the 20th Century."

Dink reached over and got a few chocolate covered peanuts to munch on while Edward sat there wondering what he was supposed to say. When he was sure Dink was finished, he asked, "That's pretty interesting, Dink. Was there a reason you brought up George Mikan today?"

When Dink had finished his snack he said, "Yes, Ed, there is. If someone as famous as George Mikan is almost totally forgotten by people, then what chance do I have of ever being remembered? A couple of weeks after I'm dead and buried, you and Sylvia will be out to dinner one night and you'll ask, 'Remember old Dink? He was a good guy wasn't he, Sylvia?' And you know what she'll say, Ed? I'll tell you what she'll say . . . 'Dink who?'"

He didn't wait for Ed to deny or object to his self-sorrowful statement. He just turned the volume on the television up loud and ate some more chocolate covered peanuts. Edward started to taste Dink's peanuts, but Dink saw Edward's hand start to move, so he grabbed the bowl and placed it on the other side of his chair. Edward got the message. As he stood up, Dink turned the volume down on the television and said, "I'll be gone for a few weeks. Not sure if I'm coming back or not. If I don't, it's been nice knowing you, Ed."

Edward was shocked. He didn't know what to say, "Where are you going? Why? What happened? Is your health okay?" Before he could decide which question to ask, there was a knock on the door and Dink said,

"Get that for me, Ed. I'm expecting someone. You take off now. And, Ed . . . take care of Sylvia."

Edward opened the door to find a middle-aged man, dressed in a suit, carrying a large briefcase. Before either the unknown man or Edward could speak, Dink yelled out, "Come on in, Seth, I don't have all day!"

Seth came in, carrying his large briefcase, and Edward walked out, wondering what in the world had just happened. Edward immediately drove over to Sylvia's house to tell her the news that Dink was leaving. He knocked on the door and Sylvia answered wearing an old pair of gym shorts and a loose fitting men's tee shirt (one that Edward had given her that read "Fiddlin' Fish"). When Edward saw the loose-fitting tee shirt on Sylvia he temporarily forgot what he had come to tell her. She planted a big hug and kiss on him, which further clouded his mind and his mission. She told him to sit down while she went to get them a glass of sweet tea.

She bounced back in the room, distracting Edward once again, and said, "Edward, do you know much about Harry Truman?" Between her bouncing ways and the news about Dink, he was incapable of answering her. So, she started, "If you recall, he wore glasses in every picture taken of him. That was because he had poor eyesight which prevented him from participating in sports. To make up for this, he started reading and playing the piano. He was proud that he had read every book in the Independence Public Library. Less than three months after he'd been elected Vice-President of the country, President Roosevelt died making him the president.

His biggest problem was that FDR had kept Truman in the dark about the war and virtually everything else. After learning about the secret atomic program, he made the decision to drop the bombs, which killed over 220,000 people. Just think of that, Edward." Oh, Edward was thinking alright. "Not long after he took office he survived an assassination attempt, which killed a White House guard. Edward . . . pay attention! He was the only president who served after 1897 without a college degree, but yet he was responsible for many profound contributions to the world society."

Sylvia scooted away from Edward so he could better concentrate, "Truman's mother was the daughter of an old Confederate family that had been briefly locked up in a Federal 'internment camp' during the Civil War. She never quite forgave either President Lincoln or the U.S. Government. Many years later, when she came to visit her son at the White House and was offered accommodations in the historic Lincoln bedroom, she said she would rather sleep on the floor 'than spend the night in the Lincoln bed.' At the age of 92, back in Independence, Mo., Mrs. Truman broke her hip when she tripped in the kitchen and the President flew out to see her. Looking up at him from her bed of pain as he walked into the room she said, 'I don't want any smart cracks out of you! I saw your picture in the paper last week putting a wreath at the Lincoln Memorial.'

You know, Edward, many people have heard of the sign President Truman kept on his desk, 'The Buck Stops Here,' but most people don't know of the other sign he kept which read, 'Always do right. This will gratify some people and astonish the rest.' When he left office, Edward, he drove himself from Washington to Missouri—just him and his wife. And his only income was his Army pension of $111.96 per month."

As Sylvia was finishing her glass of tea, Edward finally remembered why he came over. He blurted out, "Dink is leaving."

"Leaving what?"

"Leaving here . . . Arbor Acres."

Sylvia was astonished, "Where's he going?"

"I don't know."

"Why is he leaving?"

"Umm, I'm not really sure."

"Is he sick?"

"I don't think so."

"How long will he be gone?"

"I don't know."

"Edward, what DO you know?"

Edward was almost afraid to try and answer that question, "Only that he's leaving."

Sylvia stood there biting her lower lip . . . thinking. Edward was thinking that he'd like to bite her lower lip as well. Finally, Sylvia said, "What are we going to do, Edward? We can't just let him leave!"

"Why not? He's a grown man. He doesn't owe us any explanations. He can come and go as he pleases."

Sylvia didn't like that answer. She liked hers better . . ."We're going over there, Edward, and find out what's going on. What time can you pick me up in the morning?"

In the morning? Edward hoping for something more tonight. So to prolong the conversation, he asked her, "Do you know who George Mikan was, honey?"

"Of course I do, Edward. What kind of silly question is that?"

As much as Edward wanted to, he couldn't think of an answer. He was only trying to distract her until he could come up with something better.

"Pick me up at 9:30, Edward, we're gonna get to the bottom of this." After she gave that order, she turned to walk away, before saying, "Lock the door on your way out, Edward. And don't be late!"

38

EDWARD WAS RUNNING LATE and didn't get to Sylvia's house until 9:37. She was not happy! She only spoke once on the drive over to Arbor Acres, and that was to tell him to "Watch that car, Edward." When they parked, she didn't wait for Edward to come around and open the door, she hustled out and started up the walkway towards Dink's apartment, well ahead of Edward. Before arriving at the doorway, she stopped, bent over, and picked up a penny from the sidewalk. She looked at it closely then put it in her purse. By then Edward came up and opened the door for her. They walked down the corridor and took the elevator to the third floor where Dink's apartment was. Sylvia knocked on the door and looked fiercely at Edward, saying, "We're gonna get to the bottom of this."

Impatiently, she knocked a little harder. After a few moments with no movement, she knocked even harder and said in a loud voice, "Mr. Cleveland, are you in there?"

They were so focused on Dink's door that neither of them saw the door open across the hallway, where an older lady stood watching them. She said, "He's gone." Her voice startled them both. Sylvia demanded,

"Gone where?"

The old lady didn't really appreciate being interrogated in her own residence and answered, "I guess if he'd have wanted you to know, he would have told you, wouldn't he? Do you live here, honey?"

Sylvia was aghast and didn't know how to respond. The older lady then said, "Do I need to call security?"

Before Sylvia could think, Edward grabbed her arm and answered, "No, ma'am. We're leaving."

As they started down the hallway the old lady said, "Goodbye, Ed." Then quickly shut her door. They went to the receptionist's station where they found a rather plump woman eating a glazed, sprinkled doughnut. Edward asked her,

"Do you know when Mr. Cleveland will return? We came to visit him."

She slowly shook her head and replied, "No, I don't, Ed. He didn't leave any word. He sometimes does this. I'm sure he'll call you when he gets back."

Sylvia was beside herself. She asked the receptionist, "How long is he usually away? A few days? A few weeks? A month?"

The receptionist took a slow bite of her doughnut, then answered, "Yes."

"Yes, what?"

"Yes, to all of those. Sometimes longer."

Sylvia couldn't take it any longer. She turned and started back to the car. Edward smiled at the receptionist and said, "Thank you." As he turned to leave, she called out,

"Ed, I don't know where he went. He never tells us where he's going or how long he'll be away. But, I was sitting here when he left with that good-looking man in the suit and I thought I heard Mr. Cleveland say, 'Croatia.' At least I thought he said that. Sorry, I can't be more help. Was that your girlfriend?"

"Umm, yes. Sylvia. Edward scrunched up his face and said, "Croatia?"

"Yes. He also left this note for you but I didn't want to hand it to you in front of her, I didn't know who she was. As you see, it's not in an envelope or folded, so I knew what it said and I didn't want to put you in an awkward position." She handed Edward the single piece of notepaper, which read,

"Ed, I'm gone. I'll be back eventually—maybe. Unless I find something better. At any rate, don't worry about me, the function of a man is to live, not to exist. Two things I want you to know: I've instructed my lawyer to withdraw a large amount of money and give it to you. Shut up! I know what you're thinking. I have no one else to leave my money to and you're probably better than the government getting it—so shut up!

Second, I want you and Sylvia to get married . . . Now!
You'll never find any woman better than her who'll have
you. I know she loves you—she told me so. Don't dawdle
around. Run off to South Carolina or Vegas or somewhere
and do it. Quit living in sin (I know you are, she told me
that, too).

Goodbye, Edward. And thanks."

Edward read the note three times, just to make sure he
didn't miss anything. Then he looked back at the
receptionist and remembered a piece of trivia he was saving
for Dink. He started to tell her about the difference between
dolphins and porpoises. But as she took another bite of her
doughnut, Edward changed his mind and just nodded
instead. He put the note in his pocket and walked out the
door where he saw Sylvia standing by the car tapping her
foot. Before he started walking towards her he took one last
look out at the lake, over at the bench, left of the middle.

You can't do anything about the length of your life. But you can do something about its width and depth.

www.ingramcontent.com/pod-product-compliance
Lightning Source LLC
Chambersburg PA
CBHW071247210626
46818CB00013B/489